Doing My
Own Thing

Also by Nikki Carter

Step to This
It Is What It Is
It's All Good
Cool Like That
Not a Good Look
All the Wrong Moves

Published by Dafina Books

Doing My Own Thing

A Fab Life Novel

NIKKI CARTER

Dafina KTeen Books
KENSINGTON PUBLISHING CORP.
www.kensingtonbooks.com

DAFINA KTEEN BOOKS are published by

Kensington Publishing Corp.
119 West 40th Street
New York, NY 10018

All Kensington titles, imprints and distributed lines are available at special quantity discounts for bulk purchases for sales promotion, premiums, fund-raising, educational or institutional use.

Special book excerpts or customized printings can also be created to fit specific needs. For details, write or phone the office of the Kensington Special Sales Manager: Kensington Publishing Corp., 119 West 40th Street, New York, NY 10018. Attn. Special Sales Department. Phone: 1-800-221-2647.

K logo Reg. US Pat. & TM Off.
Sunburst logo Reg. US Pat. & TM Off.

ISBN-13: 978-0-7582-5558-7
ISBN-10: 0-7582-5558-6

First Printing: July 2011
10 9 8 7 6 5 4 3 2 1

Printed in the United States of America

Acknowledgments

I hate writing these. This is worse than writing the book! I want to thank so many people, but then I always leave somebody out by accident, and I spend a whole year asking for forgiveness! But anyhoo . . .

As always, I must give honor to God! He's the one who gave me the imagination to write all of these stories. My family totally rocks. Brent . . . you da best! Briahdioh, Broontyclause, Brynn-Brynn, Fatman, and Brookie-Brooke—love you!

To my editor, Mercedes Fernandez: You are such a pleasure to work with! Most of the time it doesn't feel like work at all. . . . I said MOST!

Pattie Steele-Perkins is one of the best agents in the business! If you don't know, you better ask somebody! HA! Thank you, Pattie, for all you do.

There are lots of authors who give me great advice and make me feel like I'm an author for real! Victoria, ReShonda, Eric, Rhonda, Sherri, and Dee—THANK YOU!

I've got the best Facebook crew EVER! Y'all make me laugh, motivate me, pray for me, and tell me to get the heck off the Internet and finish my stuff! Ebony, Yolanda, Ayiana, Daphine, Monica (MMJ), Zaviera, Stephanie, Michelle, and Carla—I appreciate y'all!

My besties are the ones who get the brunt of it all. They hear me stressed out on five cups of Starbucks and trying to finish a story! Afrika, Shawana, Kym, Tippy T., Robin, Brandi, and Leah—I love y'all!

And to my reader CREW. Thank you so much for asking your mama or for using your Christmas/Birthday/babysitting money to get this book. I hope there are many, many more to come!

Hope you like it!

Make it HOT!

Love,
Nikki

1

Have you ever been super nervous about something for absolutely no reason at all?

Today is the day we get to see the episodes of our BET reality show, *Backstage: The Epsilon Records Summer Tour*. I shouldn't be nervous, because I went out of my way to make sure I didn't do anything that could be misconstrued as ghetto or lame. I didn't talk bad about anybody in my confessionals, I never once used profanity, and I was only digging one boy the whole time (Sam).

So, I shouldn't be nervous.

But for some crazy reason I am. I have the butterflies-flitting-in-the-pit-of-my-stomach feeling that something ridiculous is about to pop off.

Maybe it's because I haven't really talked to anyone except Sam since the taping completed. We ended on a bad note. The final show in New York City got cancelled because of a botched kidnapping attempt that ended up in a nightclub brawl. It was all bad.

I keep playing the whole thing over and over again in my head, because I knew about the kidnapping ahead of time, but didn't tell anyone. In hindsight, I should've tried to do something, but I was afraid that something bad might happen to my mom and little cousin. That's all I was thinking about. It didn't even occur to me that telling Big D, Mystique, or Dilly about what was going down could've given a different result.

And now, I'm paying the price for that. Dilly's still not speaking to me, and the tour has been over for three weeks. Big D is a little salty with me too, and that really hurts, because he's always in my corner. Mystique is a little disappointed, but she told me that she would've done what I did, so that made me feel better.

My phone buzzes on my hip. "Hey, Sam."

"You want me to pick you up to go to the studio? Or are you driving, since you finally decided to stop being a tightwad and got yourself a car?"

I laugh out loud. Yes, I am a tightwad with the money I've earned so far on the songwriting end of things. But when I got my six-thousand-dollar check at the end of the tour, I went to a used-car lot and got a car. It's a tricked-out gold Toyota Camry that was probably seized from a drug dealer or something. Anyhoo, I'm on wheels.

"Why don't I pick you up for a change?" I ask. "I do want to drive, but I don't want to show up alone. I'm afraid I might get jumped."

"Dilly still isn't talking, huh?"

"No, and neither are Dreya and Truth, although I don't know why they're mad."

"Does Drama *need* a reason?"

I chuckle. "No, not really, but I think if someone would call her by her real name every now and then she might remember that Drama is a stage name, and that she doesn't have to live up to it."

"She will forever be Ms. Drama to me," Sam states.

"Well, whatever. She's Dreya to me. I'll pick you up in an hour. Cool?"

"Yep."

My mother calls me from the living room. "Sunday! Come here, now!"

"Sam, let me call you back. My mom is tripping on something."

Her voice sounds crazy, like she's about to try to ground me for something. But we've officially halted all punishment activities since I turned eighteen, and graduated from high school. Like how's she gonna ground me when I'm helping pay bills up in here? Real talk.

But still she sounds like she's in trip-out mode. I am sooo not in the mood.

"Sunday, sit down," my mom says when I come into the living room.

"What's up?"

"Look at what just came in the mail."

She hands me an envelope that's addressed to me and my mom, but doesn't have a return address. I open up the envelope and inside is a cashier's check.

For twenty-five thousand dollars.

It's the exact amount of money that my mother's boyfriend Carlos borrowed from my college fund to buy into Club Pyramids. It's the exact amount that was stolen from him when the deal went sour and he ended up getting shot.

"Do you think this has anything to do with Carlos's cousins trying to kidnap Dilly?" she asks.

"How can we say for sure? We don't even know who sent it."

My mother replies, "It had to be Carlos. Somehow he got his hands on the money and he's trying to make it up to you."

"But why wouldn't he let you know it was coming? I mean, he knows how to get in contact with us."

My mother sits down next to me and takes the check back. She flips it over a few times as if she's looking for clues to its origin. She sighs and shakes her head.

"Maybe it was the record company. Maybe they want all of the ghettoness surrounding you to stop, especially since they want to do a reality show with just you."

Apparently, BET liked what they saw of me from the reality-show footage, and they want to give me my own show. That's all good, and I know they don't want any more brawls taking place during my new gig. But how would the head honchos at BET know about the twenty-five thousand dollars? There is no way Mystique or Big D would tell them what *really* went down at the club in New York.

"I don't think it was Epsilon Records, Mommy. They aren't really in the loop with all the drama."

"Maybe it was Big D or Mystique?"

I bite my lip and think about this for a moment. Big D is out. He's known all along about the money, and if he wanted to give it to me, he could've done it at any time. Mystique is a possibility. She's the type who would do something under the radar and not sign her name to it.

"I don't know," I finally reply. "Maybe. I'll ask them both."

My mother shakes her head. "No. Don't ask. Whoever sent this doesn't want it to be known, or else they would've signed their name. We just have to look at it for exactly what it is."

"And what's that?" I ask, completely confused at her reasoning.

"That's simple. It's a gift from God."

Hmmm . . . a gift from God? While I'm as Christian as the next person, I doubt that He's just sending random checks in the mail. If He was doing that, why doesn't He send them to people who really need it? I mean, for real, I've got hundreds of thousands of dollars on the way. Isn't there some poor single mom out there who could use the check more? I'm just saying.

But there's no way I'm gonna argue with my mother when it has to do with a blessing. She'll make me attend daily revivals, Bible study, vacation Bible school and everything else if I even think I sound like I don't have faith.

So, it's up to me to figure out the identity of the mystery check writer. Something new to put on my already overflowing plate!

"Well, I guess we just need to thank the Lord," I reply.

"You sound like you're being sarcastic, Sunday."

"I'm not! If it's from God, then I think I should thank Him."

"All right. Keep it up and your new reality show will follow you around at vacation Bible school."

This would be funny only if she didn't really mean it. Even though I'm eighteen, I'm still afraid of her. I have to hurry up and figure out who the mystery check donor is, before my mom makes her move.

Can somebody say a prayer for me?

2

When Sam and I step through the studio door and into Big D's tricked-out lounge, the tension is pretty thick. Dreya and Truth are sitting on one end of Big D's new white leather couch, and Shelly is chilling in one of the four huge, fluffy, white leather armchairs. Bethany is huddled on the other end of the couch and Dilly is at her feet on the floor, on a large pillow.

Everyone seems to be waiting for something. And the facial expressions are beyond stressed.

"You redecorated," I comment to Big D.

"Shelly wanted to do all white and a big-screen TV, since Big D in the A Records is in the TV business now."

"I know that's right! After our show airs on BET, it's gonna be on and poppin'. They're gonna sign us up for like ten seasons," Dreya said.

Big D and I exchange glances. Apparently, he hasn't told

Dreya about my reality show. I already know there's gonna be some mess behind this.

"But, I think before we even talk about that, we need to watch this DVD of our tour show. The one that's about to premiere on BET next Friday," Big D says.

Truth says, "Did you already watch it?"

"Yeah, and for the most part, I think y'all are gonna be cool with how it turned out."

Bethany lifts her right eyebrow suspiciously. "For the most part? What does that mean?"

"I don't think you have to worry," Dreya says with a laugh. "The show isn't about you."

"Ladies, please," Big D says in his exasperated voice. "Let's just watch the DVD."

Sam says, "What? No popcorn?"

"I know, right!" I add, hearing my stomach growl.

Big D replies, "I've got food on the way. Pizza, wings, pasta, and soda. It should be here soon."

Big D walks over to the big-screen television and pops the DVD into a slot on the side. Sam and I both plop down into big leather armchairs. He takes the one closest to Dilly, and Bethany and I sit down nearest to the TV.

I look over at Dilly out of the corner of my eye. He's still mean mugging like nobody's business. We've got to get a resolution to this beef quick, fast, and in a hurry because I'm not working with him if he's gonna hold grudges.

"What is it with you, dude? Why you keep looking at Sunday all like that?" Sam asks, as if reading my mind. "You gonna have to fall back with all that madness."

Dilly lets out a wicked-sounding laugh. "You her bodyguard or something?"

"You want to find out?" Sam replies.

"I'm supposed to be grinnin' and cheesin' at someone who almost got me kidnapped? How does that make any sense?"

I jump up out of my chair and scream at the top of my lungs. "How many times do I have to apologize to you, dude? You act like I'm the one who put together that plot! You should feel lucky we even deal with you at all, the way your brother and sister have threatened my family."

Big D steps to Dilly and intervenes. "Listen here, son. The only reason you're in my camp is because Sunday and Mystique spoke up for you. Epsilon is really feelin' Sunday right now, so what's good for her is good for Big D in the A Records. Ya' feel me?"

Dilly nods. "Yeah. I feel you."

"You start making her feel uncomfortable," Big D continues, "then you're making me uncomfortable. And I'm not about to feel that way up in *my* spot, ya' dig?"

"Oh my God!" Dreya shouts. "She ain't the queen bee up in here! If dude is mad, so-freaking-be-it! Can we watch the video? I'm ready for my close-up!"

Leave it to Dreya to bring everybody's attention back to her. And I don't recall ever acting like I was the queen bee of anything. That was a true hater comment if I ever heard one.

"My baby's ready to see herself on TV," Truth says as he kisses Dreya's neck.

My eyes widen a little when I see Dreya pull away from Truth as he tries to kiss her. It's a very small and subtle move that I would've missed if I wasn't glaring in Dreya's direction. Something is up between Dreya and Truth. I wonder if she knows about his and Bethany's extracurricular hookups while we were on tour. But, no, she couldn't possibly know about it, because Bethany is still her roomie.

Big D presses Play on his remote and our reality show's opening sequence plays over music from my album. It's my first single, "Can U See Me."

I hear Dreya inhale a sharp breath and her eyebrows furrow into a tight frown. Houston, we've got a problem. For real.

I don't think it would be so bad if the opening sequence didn't have me posted up front and center, like the show is all about me and everybody else is my supporting cast. Dreya's and Truth's images are in the background right with Sam, Bethany, Big D, Shelly, Dilly, and Ms. Layla.

The last shot is some footage of me and Mystique where she puts her arm around me and hands me a microphone. I remember us goofing off and doing these poses in front of the BET cameras. I don't think anyone, most of all me, knew that this would be the end result.

Dreya looks madder than a bunch of hoodrats ready to fight over the last bulk of platinum yaki weave.

I take a deep breath as we go into the episodes. . . .

Episode 1

All is cool in the beginning of this episode. The cameras show shots of the tour bus—the outside and inside. There's much footage of Dreya in diva mode, demanding cans of Sprite, extra pillows—her usual. They've got Aunt Charlie dancing, booty popping, and rump shaking. Everybody laughs out loud, even Dreya, when Aunt Charlie blows a kiss at the cameraman.

Next, there's a confessional with me, and I say, "I feel cool about going on tour with Truth."

After they show that sound bite, they cut to a shot of Dreya marching around the bus, making demands. Then they cut back to my confessional.

"There's no beef. We're first cousins." I see my face smiling at me on the TV screen.

Immediately, I notice that these two sound bites are from two different confessionals. My hair isn't even the same in the two shots. Next, there are confessionals from Dreya and Truth.

Dreya says, "Sunday wasn't supposed to be on this tour, but it's whatever. I'm the star and she's my opening act. . . . So it's whatever. We can all eat, right?"

I roll my eyes hard over in Dreya's direction. She's tripping! I can see right now, I was probably the only one trying to keep it positive on this reality show.

Truth's little sound bite isn't any better. "Sunday is . . . well, you know . . . she be playin' games and stuff. Ain't no beef at all. Her dude is even with us on tour. It's all gravy."

I glare at Truth and Dreya and holler over the TV. "I'm playin' games? What the heck are you on?"

Truth laughs. "Girl, watch the show!"

I fold my arms across my chest and slump down into the soft leather chair. For the record, I do not like Truth or Dreya.

Episode 2

This show flashes back to me and Dreya trying on stage costumes at Ms. Layla's studio, and us learning choreography at Mystique's dance studio. I see that they don't mind showing stuff out of sequence.

The next shot is of Dreya in the confessional booth. She says, "Mystique's mama has absolutely no fashion sense at all. I can't believe I have to wear these ugly spandex unitards on my first tour! Why everybody got to be a fashion designer? I heard she used to be a caterer or some mess, but her daughter gets a record deal and all of a sudden she's a designer? Not!"

My jaw drops! I can't believe Dreya would go in on Ms. Layla like that. Can somebody say career suicide? Mystique is the number-one chick in the game right now, and there's nothing Dreya can do about that. She doesn't even qualify as Mystique's competition.

I cringe when they show a conversation that Dreya and I had at Mystique's studio about Sam and our whole prom fiasco.

She'd asked me about what happened and my answer was, "He didn't play me. I uninvited him. It's all good."

Then these dang editors skipped the most important part of the conversation where I deny ever pushing up on Truth at the club (which is what started the entire prom fiasco). The next sound bite is Dreya saying, "I'm just saying, why Sam is not checking for you. But Dilly is. He's cute, but . . . you know."

Totally uncomfortable in here right now. Sam is looking all kinds of crazy and Dilly has nothing to say about Dreya's compliment. He could've at least said thank you.

Episode 3

This is the prom episode! I sit back and relax myself, because even though I didn't go with Sam, my dress, hair, and nails are fiyah!

"We look good, Sunday!" Dreya gives me a high five in the air. I throw her one back.

Whose idea was it for us to watch this together? Now Dilly's got a smirk on his face, Bethany is all twisted up, and Sam has this glazed-over look on his face. This is all bad. I need the escape hatch right about now.

I didn't think this could get worse, but it does.

Up on the TV screen Dilly spins me around and says his little freestyle. *"I wish I had a million bucks, I do in my head/But I'd take a million of your kisses instead."*

Then, they show Sam touching my shoulder and telling me to have fun. I don't remember his face looking so sad when he said that, but I'm seeing it now live and in color. Finally the scene ends with Dilly putting his arm around me and whispering in my ear.

I know that Dilly was making me feel better about not going to the prom with Sam, but nobody in the viewing audience could hear that!

"Sunday . . ." Sam says. "For real?"

Sam gets up and storms out! I get up and follow him, because I can't let him think something crazy.

"Pause that, Big D. I'll be right back."

"Drama!" Dreya hollers out with a laugh. I could smack her straight upside the head.

When I finally catch up to Sam he's standing outside Big D's house, bent over with his hands on his knees and panting like he just ran a marathon.

I run up behind him, my flip-flops slapping on the marble tiles. "Sam, please let me explain."

"It really looks like you were digging Dilly. I feel like such an idiot," Sam says.

"Listen, Dilly did me a favor by not letting me look like a lame at my prom. That's all there was to it."

Sam turns to face me. "Sunday, come on. He was freestyling about a million of your kisses."

"That was for the BET cameras, Sam! I promise."

"So how many did he get?"

"How many what?" Then my eyes widen with disbelief. "Oh, come on! Are you serious, Sam?"

"I'm dead serious. How many kisses did he get that night? How much more than that did he get?"

I puff air into my cheeks and blow it out all at once, probably giving Sam a good whiff of my grape-scented breath.

"I did not kiss him, Sam! But how are you gonna be mad? Did you kiss Rielle at your prom?"

Sam is silent for an extra-long moment.

"I thought so. You're tripping with this double-standard stuff, Sam. For real."

"I didn't kiss her," Sam replies. "I thought about you the whole night."

Even though most boys lie about this kind of thing, I believe Sam.

"So what are we gonna do?" I ask.

He shrugs and turns back toward Big D's mansion and reaches for the door. "Right now, we're gonna go finish watching this reality show. Then, after that . . . I don't know what."

"Why don't we play it by ear?" I ask as I walk through the door Sam holds for me.

"Yeah. Okay."

Whoever said that girls bring more drama than boys totally has it twisted. Sam is full of drama! He's worse than a chick.

Everyone stares at us as we come back into the room.

"What y'all lookin' at?" Sam asks with attitude.

Big D laughs out loud. "You run out the room like a little diva and then you wanna ask who's looking at you? I thought you wanted us to look at you."

Sam snatches a couch pillow that was lying next to Shelly and throws it at Big D. Big D jumps up from his seat and puts Sam in a fake headlock.

"You straight, dog?" Big D asks.

"Yeah, I'm straight."

Big D presses Play and we watch the rest of the episode. One positive thing I can say is that they leave out the fight between Aunt Charlie and Dilly's older sister LaKeisha. I guess that was too ghetto for prime time.

Episode 4

The scene starts with Dreya bossing Bethany around right before a concert. Dreya tells Bethany to "make herself useful and find her a can of Sprite." Dreya doesn't even look at Bethany as she gives the command. If she had, she would've seen the hateful look on Bethany's face.

Then they cut to a confessional of Bethany. She's in tears, so I already know it's gonna be all bad.

On the television screen, a pitiful-looking Bethany dabs at her eyes with a tissue. "We all used to be best friends, you know? Me, Drama, and Sunday. We were a girl group and we were supposed to blow up together! Now, Drama acts like I'm her slave. I'm only doing this so I can get a record deal."

Dreya jumps up and grabs the remote control from Big D and presses Pause. "I do not treat you like a slave. I treat you like you're my assistant. I can't believe you got on national TV and tried to make me out to be some kind of diva, 'cause I asked your ungrateful behind to get me a can of Sprite. That's the *least* you could do."

"It's not what you ask," Bethany says. "It's *how* you ask. You've got a really stank attitude, Drama. For real."

"Can we just finish watching it?" Truth says.

Dreya hands the remote back to Big D, and sashays back to her seat next to Truth. "You're just jealous, Bethany. If I get on your nerves so bad, you can get out of my apartment."

Bethany doesn't reply to this. She slumps back in her seat, folds her arms, and pouts like a toddler.

"I'm for real, Bethany, you can get out. I don't need you up in my spot anyway killing my vibe with all your hatin'. Pack your bags, Ma."

Bethany storms out of the room and Dilly follows her. Dreya bursts into laughter as she snuggles up next to Truth.

"Nobody cares if she's mad. Come on, Big D. Press Play."

Episode 5

This episode has more concert footage. They show the concert where the heel of Dreya's shoe broke, and the one where my mic wasn't working. They even include Dilly's freestyle, which to me was super hot. Too bad he's off comforting Bethany.

Then, there is some dramatic footage of Truth's arrest. I'd forgotten how scared we all were until I see everyone's faces on the television screen. No one looks more terrified than Truth.

"I believe that Truth is innocent," I say in my on-screen confessional. "This is just a big mess."

I remember doing that confessional. It was the day after Truth got arrested. He was in jail in South Carolina, and Dreya and Big D had stayed behind to bail him out. It was an intense time for everybody, but Mystique pretty much saved the day.

There's a confessional with Mystique too. "It's really unfortunate what's happened with Truth. I just hope we can get back to the positive things we're doing with this tour. Sunday is really a positive artist! She's got star quality."

Dreya stands to her feet and roars. "WHAT! What is she doing on our show giving Sunday props? Big D, you had something to do with this, I know. You're so thirsty for Mystique to throw a little shine your way."

The television continues to play in the background like a soundtrack to Dreya's meltdown.

"That's not true, but if you want to believe it, I'm not about to argue with you," Big D says. "Are you going to sit down so we can finish watching this?"

Dreya ignores Big D's question. "And Sunday. Don't nobody need you defending my man. We all knew he was innocent. Nobody asked your little goody-two-shoe self!"

"Someone did ask me! The BET producer asked what I thought. You trippin', Dreya." I respond in a heated tone. She's starting to work my nerves.

Truth pulls Dreya's arm. "Come on now, babe. A blind man could see what's going on here. Mystique, Epsilon, BET, and all of them are trying to blow Sunday up. But it's all good. She can't take your shine."

Oh no, he didn't.

I know Truth doesn't want me to tell Dreya all about his secret lip-locking sessions with Bethany. Let him get out of pocket concerning me one more time, and he's gonna get put all the way on blast.

Dreya turns to Truth and smiles. "You got that right, baby. Sunday and her Disney looks and lyrics ain't got nothing on me."

Dreya and Truth get up to leave the room. She makes sure to swing her behind in my face on her way out. I know she's my family, but sometimes I really can't stand her. But as soon as she sees Bethany and Dilly making their way back into the room, Dreya and Truth stop in their tracks.

Bethany plops back down on the leather couch and Dilly reclaims his spot at her feet.

"You done licking your wounds?" Dreya asks.

Bethany ignores her, and folds her arms across her chest.

Dreya leans forward in her chair and snakes her neck

real hard. "I know you not trying to ignore me! Do you know who I am?"

Bethany does not reply, but throws Big D a glance. "Can you please press Play?"

"Ooh, you better be glad I just got my nails done!" Dreya says.

Episodes 6 & 7

These two episodes are actually kind of boring compared to the previous episodes—which is a good thing because everybody's looking uncomfortable and edgy.

A beeping noise comes from the kitchen. Hopefully, it has something to do with the delicious smells that keep wafting toward my nose.

Shelly says, "Y'all want something to eat? The lasagna is ready."

"Yeah, we better pause here anyway. They need a break before the next episode."

Everyone looks at Big D. I, for one, want an explanation of what he just said. You can't drop a bomb like that and then just go and eat lasagna like ain't nothing twisted.

"Forget the lasagna," Dreya says. "Turn the TV back on, Big D."

"Trust me on this one. Take a break and get your head right, Drama."

"Do I need to start blowing up in here?" Dreya asks. "Ain't nothing you can do to calm me down now."

I say, "Yeah, Big D. You've got us all stressed out now. We might as well watch it and get it over with."

Big D chews the toothpick hanging out of his mouth. "All right then. Sit down and buckle your seat belts. It's about to get a little bumpy."

Episode 8

The episode starts out innocently enough. It's footage from my graduation reception at Applebee's. Everybody looks like they're having fun on camera, except Dreya, but that's understandable because she didn't graduate. She's still working with a tutor to get that last English credit.

Then it cuts to a Bethany confessional. Immediately, I can tell that something isn't right because of the look of horror on Bethany's face, both on the TV screen and sitting here in Big D's living room.

On-screen, she clears her throat. "First of all, I'm only on this tour because I want a record deal. I can't stand Dreya anymore."

Dreya jumps up. "What?"

"Sit down. There's more," Big D says as he waves his hand dismissively in Dreya's direction.

The confessional continues. "Yeah, I knew she wasn't gonna graduate. That's what happens when you cheat on your final. You get a zero."

The on-screen Bethany bursts into laughter. "*Someone*, let's just say, a little birdie, told our English teacher that someone was selling her final exam, and what do you know? She changed it at the last minute."

This time when Dreya jumps up from her seat, she

lunges toward Bethany. Truth pulls her back down. Big D presses Pause . . . again.

"Drama, it's cool. You wasn't gonna get to cross the stage anyway," Truth says.

Dreya rolls her eyes and tries to snatch herself out of Truth's grip. "That's not the point! This chick is supposed to be my friend and she ratted me out?"

"I didn't hear that she ratted you out," I say. I'm trying to keep the peace, but it's kind of hard with Bethany sitting up here grinning, the scared look gone from her face.

"Yeah, I ratted you out. I sure did! And what?" Bethany spits words across the room at Dreya like she done lost every piece of her mind.

"Bethany, I think you need to roll out," Big D says. "After this next part, I don't think even I can hold her back from beating you down."

"I ain't scared of her!" Bethany screams. "Press Play, Big D!"

Big D shakes his head. "I don't think you're understanding. Bounce, right now, Bethany. Dilly, take your girl and roll!"

Big D's menacing facial expression doesn't leave them much of an option. He looks like a big ol' scary genie with his bald head, dark goatee, and hoop earring. He'd almost be a black version of that cat on the Mr. Clean bottle if his stomach wasn't so big.

"Come on, Bethany," Dilly says. "I'm tired of being over here anyway."

"I want to see the rest of it," Bethany says. "I'm ready for my close-up too, why you playin'."

"You'll see it when it airs," Big D says.

I guess it's pretty clear to everyone that Big D is not budging. Bethany and Dilly stand to leave.

"Get your stuff out of my apartment," Dreya says. "I ain't playing either. If I come home and your stuff is still in my apartment, I'm throwing it in the middle of the street."

"Gladly. I wasn't planning on living with you anymore anyway," Bethany replies.

"Wait, y'all," I say. "You're just mad now. Maybe, once you cool off, you won't feel the same way."

"I'm not mad at all," Bethany says. "I can't stand her."

"Ditto!" Dreya screams.

"Come on, Bethany," Dilly repeats. "Let's just go."

Bethany cocks her head to one side and looks at me. "Sunday, don't forget your promise. I did what you asked, so now you've got to keep your promise."

She would be referring to the promise I made to her that I'd help her with her album if she stopped creeping with Truth on the tour. I think she was more scared than anything that I was going to tell Dreya and that she wasn't going to be able to get her record done before getting voted out of the group.

"I don't *have* to do anything, but I will because I said I would. But I think you should leave now. For real."

Bethany tosses her long, brown hair over one shoulder and rakes her hand through it a few times to make it lay flat. She takes one last look at Dreya while running her tongue over her silver lip ring.

"What are you looking at?" Dreya asks.

Bethany doesn't answer, she just laughs and walks away, with Dilly on her heels.

When the door shuts behind them, Big D presses Play again.

The next piece of footage is backstage at a concert. I remember this. This was when . . .

OMG!

I thought the cameras hadn't captured this! On-screen, Bethany sneaks into a closet, and moments later Truth joins her. The footage is dark and grainy, like an episode of *Cheaters*, but you could still tell that it's Bethany and Truth!

Then there's some more of Bethany's confessional. "He's gonna help me get a record deal, so it's whatever."

Truth is sitting up in his seat, in total shock. Clearly the BET producer hadn't asked *him* about his hooking up with Bethany.

"I'm gonna beat the dog slop out of that alley rat," Dreya says.

Truth touches Dreya's arm and she snatches it away. "Don't touch me!" she screams at the top of her lungs. "You're just as bad as she is!"

When Truth opens his mouth to speak, Dreya hauls off and slaps his face—hard enough to make his nose bleed. Truth touches the blood with a look of surprise on his face.

Suddenly (although it feels like it's going in slow motion), Truth shoves Dreya hard in the middle of her chest. Her breath comes out with an *oomph* sound as she flies into Big D's white marble coffee table.

"Hey!" Big D says. "That's enough. You ain't gonna be manhandling your girl up in my crib."

Truth laughs. "She should learn to keep her hands to herself. You ain't see her slap me?"

I shake my head in total awe of what's playing out right before my eyes. My mother and Aunt Charlie have always told me and Dreya to never hit boys. I can almost hear my mother's voice in my head right now. *He might hit back, and I guarantee he'll be stronger than you are.*

Truth wipes the still-dripping blood with the back of his hand. He goes downstairs to the studio portion of Big D's house, and Dreya sits on the floor with tears running down her face.

"Dreya, are you okay?" Yeah, I was just mad at her like fifty-two seconds ago, but in an emergency, Tollivers roll deep.

She closes her eyes and gives a little dismissive head shake. "Of course I'm okay. He barely touched me. I just tripped, that's all."

Okay, that's not what I saw, but it seems Dreya wants to believe some crazy edited version of the truth.

Big D says, "Why don't we just watch the rest of this later? I knew y'all was gonna be mad, but dang . . ."

"Just go, Sunday," Dreya says with a small, trembling voice. She sounds like she's fighting really hard to keep from crying.

"Do you want me to drive you home?" I ask. I don't feel one-hundred-percent comfortable about leaving her here with Truth.

"No. And don't tell my mother about this. I don't want her coming up here overreacting."

The last time I kept an important secret like this, Dilly almost wound up kidnapped, and he could've been murdered. So, I don't care what Dreya says. I'm telling Aunt Charlie all about this thing.

Big D says, "Look, Sunday, I'll make sure she gets home okay."

I hesitate for a moment longer, not sure if I trust Big D to handle this situation and his boy, Truth, properly. It's in Big D's best interest for all of this to go away and get swept under the rug. I don't think Epsilon Records would be cool with this at all.

"Okay," I finally say. "But Dreya, you better call me if Truth puts his hands on you again."

"He won't. Stop blowing this out of proportion," Dreya says with an irritated tone in her voice.

How in the world is she irritated with someone worrying about her simple behind? She gets on my nerves.

As an afterthought, I add, "And you might want to fall back with all that slapping too."

3

Sam and I ride in silence as we head home from Big D's studio. Sam not talking is always a bad thing because it means he's either brooding or mad about something. I'm not trying to have the "Sunday, be my girlfriend" conversation again! It makes me weary. So before he goes there, I'm gonna steer him elsewhere.

"You want to go over my house and watch a movie or something?" I ask.

"Chick flick or action?"

"I was thinking action. *Wolverine* to be exact."

"Is your Aunt Charlie there?" Sam asks.

"Probably. Is that a deal breaker?"

He laughs out loud. "She and Manny are funny! I love hanging out with them."

"Aunt Charlie is funny. She's gonna be so happy about being on the reality show. This is gonna be like a dream

come true for her. Do you think it's gonna be a hit?" I ask
Sam as I pull onto I-20.

Sam runs a hand over his low fade and licks his lips.
That's a habit he has, something he does when he's thinking. It's one of my favorites of Sam's little tics. The cutest
one, at least.

"I think it will be a hit," Sam says, "but at what cost?
Drama and Truth seem like they're over."

I drum my fingers on the steering wheel as I come to a
complete stopping point on the freeway. This Atlanta
traffic is madness during rush hour. We should've waited
before we left Big D's house.

"I don't think they're over. They're too perfect for each
other."

"Maybe you're right," Sam concurs. "But what's going
on with Bethany and Dilly? I didn't know they'd gotten
that close."

"Yeah, they kind of did after the tour."

Before the kidnapping attempt, Dilly had not been shy
about his crush on me. He hadn't pushed all the way up,
but he always let it be known that he was catching feelings. But after Los Diablos, when Carlos's gangsta cousins
tried to snatch Dilly from the club, he'd decided to return
Bethany's attention. They don't seem like a match to
me. . . . But hey, what do I know?

"This is what I can't figure out," Sam says. "If he hates
you so much and she hates Drama, why do they even
come around? It's not like Big D even wants them there."

I ponder this for a long moment. We're not going anywhere for a while in this gridlocked traffic, so I've got

plenty of time to put on my thinking cap as we creep on I-20, inching toward my exit.

"They just want to blow up. Going through us is probably the easiest route to do that."

Sam nods in agreement. "Yeah, I can see that. Are you still gonna help Bethany with her album? Since Drama knows about Bethany and Truth, doesn't that kind of mean that the arrangement is off?"

"Well, I promised her I'd help if she stopped messing with Truth. It didn't really have anything to do with Dreya finding out. I promised I wouldn't tell, but I guess she should've sworn the BET producers to secrecy too."

This makes me think of Truth putting his hands on Dreya, and I feel myself get angry all over again. I feel myself grip the steering wheel in frustration as I finally get off on the Candler Road exit.

"Can you believe that Truth pushed Dreya like that? It looked like he was really trying to hurt her."

Sam's face scrunches into a frown. "I don't think he was trying to hurt her. But why would she just slap him like that?"

"I agree that she shouldn't have slapped him, but are you saying that makes it okay for him to retaliate like he did?"

Sam shrugs, and points across the road at Captain D's. "Can you stop and get something to eat? We never did get any of Shelly's lasagna."

My stomach growls in agreement.

We roll through the Captain D's drive-thru and order

two ten-piece family value packs, with fries and cole slaw. Twenty pieces of fish ought to be enough for any and everybody who might appear at our house.

While we're waiting for our food (why do I always have to pull forward and wait when I come here? Why don't they keep cooking fish like all night? Don't they know I'm hungry? AARGH!), Sam looks over at me like he wants to say something deep.

I cannot handle him being deep on an empty stomach.

Sam says, "Sunday, you be playing games."

"How so? What are you talking about?"

"I'm just thinking of how it seemed like you had Dilly twisted and crushing hard on you, and then you just blew him off."

OMG! What is this fool tripping on? I blew Dilly off because I knew Sam's little sensitive butt would be mad. I must admit that when I first saw Dilly, I thought he was fiyah, but that was it. And plus, Dilly is younger than me. I wasn't about to be boo'ed up with him!

"I never planned on talking to Dilly. I didn't have him twisted."

Sam laughs. "No, for real, check out. You had Truth chasing behind you, and me taking you to aquariums and other assorted bull crap, and you ain't checking for nobody."

"We went on another date, didn't we?" I ask.

After the tour, Sam and I had a great time on our one date. We went out to dinner at Justin's and even got the VIP treatment once the waitress recognized me. That was hot!

"Exactly. One date, and you acted like you were doing me a favor the whole time."

"No, I didn't. I just didn't commence any follow-up activities," I explain. "You know I've got to do this reality show thing with just me. It's crazy right now."

Sam chuckles sadly as we take our food from the Captain D's worker. "One of these days I'm gonna stop begging you, Sunday."

I don't answer him as I drive off from the restaurant and head toward my house. I believe that he's not going to wait around forever, for me to make up my mind. I don't think it'll take forever, though. I like Sam, I've just got work to do. People to see, places to go . . . you know.

Sam's brooding look has evaporated by the time we pull into my driveway. This is good, because I don't want to watch a movie with him sulking and glaring at me out of the corner of his eye.

When I open the front door, my five-year-old cousin, Manny, is standing in the living room eating a hot dog—his treat of choice. I hold up the bags from Captain D's and he drops his hot dog on the floor.

"You coulda told a brotha you was bringing some food, Sunday!" Manny fusses.

I put the food on the table, pick Manny up, and kiss him on the cheek. "Hush all your noise, little boy."

"Get me a plate, Sunday," Aunt Charlie says from the couch. She's drinking a can of Pepsi. This is her new thing since she gave up cigarettes right after our tour. She said that she thought the cigarettes were making her look old, and if her daughter was going to be on TV, then she couldn't be looking all geriatric.

"Okay, Auntie. Is my mother here?"

"Naw. She's working overtime. Somebody called in sick and she volunteered to help carry their mail route."

Sidebar. I can't wait until I make enough money so that my mother doesn't have to carry mail anymore! She works so hard, and something on her always hurts. Her back, feet, knees, ankles . . . I just want her to sit at home and chill, sipping tea and watching movies.

"Hello, Ms. Tolliver," Sam says politely as he takes a seat at the table next to Manny.

"Ms. Tolliver? I'm Charlie, baby. Ms. Tolliver is my sister."

Sam laughs out loud. "Can I call you Ms. Charlie? I don't feel right calling a grown lady by her first name."

"I guess I can roll with Ms. Charlie. Where y'all coming from?"

"Big D's studio. We were watching the reality show DVD," I reply as I place a plate of fish, hush puppies, fries, and coleslaw in front of Manny.

"Why you ain't tell me! I wanted to see it too. Did I look fly?"

Sam replies, "Ms. Charlie, you were hella fine."

"That's what I'm talking about!" Aunt Charlie stands up and does a little dance where she drops her booty halfway to the floor and pops back up.

Blank stare. Like mother, like daughter!

"Aunt Charlie, can I ask you about a hypothetical situation?" I ask, thinking about how I'm gonna tell her about Dreya.

"Hypothetical? Hmmm . . . yeah, go ahead."

I clear my throat and walk over to Aunt Charlie. I hand her the plate that I've fixed for her.

"What would you say . . . if a guy . . . hypothetically . . . pushed his girlfriend to the ground and knocked the wind out of her?"

Sam's eyes grew large. "Sunday . . ."

I give him the hand. I'm telling my aunt about this. I don't care what Dreya says.

"This boy putting his hands on you?" Aunt Charlie jumps up and lunges toward Sam.

"Auntie, no!" I shout. "I'm not talking about Sam. I said it was a hypothetical situation."

"Mmm-hmmm . . ." says Aunt Charlie, not totally convinced.

"So would it be okay for the boy to do that if the girlfriend . . . hypothetically . . . slapped her boyfriend in the face?"

Aunt Charlie chews her hush puppy and swallows it before answering. "Well, why did she slap him?"

"She found out he was cheating on her with a friend. Hypothetically."

"Oh, will you stop saying hypothetically!" Aunt Charlie fussed. "If you're not talking about yourself then you must be talking about Dreya. That little dred-head boy is cheating on my daughter? Who he messin' with?"

"Ummmm . . . Bethany."

Aunt Charlie stands to her feet and throws her hands in the air. "I told Dreya that girl was a snake! I knew it!"

"Something like that," Sam says, "but Truth isn't innocent here either."

"Yeah, I know. Especially if he thinks he can put his hands on my daughter and live to tell about it. I'm fixing to call Pookie and them."

I roll my eyes. We do not have anyone in our family named Pookie.

"Well, while you calling Pookie, do you mind if we put a movie in? You always hogging the TV."

Manny looks up from his plate with bright eyes and a huge smile. "What are we watching?"

"*We* are watching *Wolverine*. You are going to sleep, little man," I reply.

Manny's smile turns all the way upside down. "Why you tryin' to play me? I like movies."

Aunt Charlie pulls out her cell phone from the strap on her tank top. Yeah, that's where she used to keep her pack of cigarettes before she quit. I guess she feels naked without a square-shaped object on her shoulder. Blank. Stare.

"Dreya!" she screams into the phone. "Do I need to come up to that studio? I will beat the mess out of Big D and that little dredded-out thug."

Sam covers his mouth to stifle a laugh. Me too. I'm imagining Aunt Charlie trying to go up against Big D. That would not be a good look for her!

"She hung up on me!" Aunt Charlie fumes as she starts pressing buttons on the phone again.

"Do you think we're going to get to watch the movie?" I whisper to Sam.

He laughs and shakes his head. "No . . ."

Finally, Aunt Charlie presses End on her phone and places it back underneath her tank strap. "So, Sunday, when you say he put his hands on her, was she hurt?"

"No, I don't think she was hurt. It was just the way that he did it."

Aunt Charlie shakes her head and paces the floor angrily. "I keep telling her about those thuggish boys."

"Big D said he'd make sure she got home safely. She wouldn't leave with me," I say.

"Yeah, well, Big D better hope nothing happens to my daughter."

I reply, "I think we're all hoping that nothing happens to Dreya."

Sam nods slowly. I see him eyeing the TV as he chomps on another fish fillet. With Aunt Charlie this riled up, we might as well leave.

"Sam, you want to go to your house and work on some music?"

"Yeah, we can. Especially since we've got that new project that you signed us up for."

I narrow my eyes into little slits. I don't need Aunt Charlie to know that we're working on Bethany's album. She would not take too kindly to that right about now.

I reply through clenched teeth. "Let's just go, Sam."

"Can I finish my food, bossy girl?" he asks.

I just shake my head and throw my hand into the air. I sit down on the couch next to Sam after grabbing a plate with a couple of fish fillets and some fries.

"Y'all tell Truth, I'm gonna hurt him when I see him," Aunt Charlie fusses.

"Auntie, I don't think Dreya would want you to do that. Is my mom coming home after work?"

"She says she is going on a date when she gets off."

I choke on the piece of food that I just put into my mouth. My mother, on a date? My mother is still in love with Carlos.

"With . . . who?" I say between coughs.

"Some guy on her job that's been asking her for months. She finally decided to say yes."

"But what about Carlos?"

Aunt Charlie shrugs. "I don't know. I think she got tired of waiting on him to come back. He's in New York with those cousins of his, and he ain't thinking about your mother enough to even keep in touch on a regular."

Yeah, I don't understand why he can't keep in touch. After the threat Los Diablos put on Dilly's life, Bryce and LaKeisha have been laying pretty low. I guess now that the drama is at their doorstep, they're not trying to bring it as hard.

I wipe my greasy hands on a paper towel and toss the rest of my food into the trash bin. "You ready now, Sam?"

"Yes, let's go make some more paper."

"That's what I'm talking about! Aunt Charlie, can you tell my mom that if I make it home before her, then we're gonna have some things to talk about in the morning?"

Aunt Charlie ignores my joke and starts tapping numbers on the phone again. She looks really worried, and it makes me second-guess my decision to tell her about Truth putting his hands on Dreya.

But Dreya is my cousin . . . and I love her.

So, even if she thinks she knows what's best for her, I know that Aunt Charlie is gonna make it do what it do. Then my work is done, and all is well.

Well, maybe not *all* will be well. I definitely don't think that everything will be cool with Truth after Aunt Charlie gets done.

4

"What kind of sound are we giving Bethany?" Sam asks as he absentmindedly taps keys on his keyboard.

We're in the living room of his house, and we're the only ones here. His mom is working late, as usual, and no one lives here except the two of them. Must be nice. I remember how peaceful it used to be when it was just me and my mom.

The house stayed clean, the dishes stayed washed, when I put a bottle of juice in the refrigerator, it was there when I returned. Ahhh . . . the memories.

"I don't know. Bethany's voice is kind of gravelly and soulful," I say, finally answering his question. "She's got a lot of power on her lower-register notes. A lot of girls aren't able to pull those off and keep their tonal quality."

Sam chuckles. "I love it when you talk shop."

I take a couch pillow and hurl it at him. "You know what I mean! She's got a good voice."

"So, you thinking a white Alicia Keys?" Sam asks.

"Nah, I'm thinking a white Joss Stone."

Sam cracks up laughing. "Sunday, Joss Stone is white!"

"You know what I mean!" I scream again. There are no other couch pillows to throw, so I just glare over at him.

"So we're talking soulful ballads, and mid-tempo stuff?" Sam asks.

"That sounds about right."

"I can't believe we're really doing this. As down as you are for your cousin, and she was messing with your cousin's man. I mean, I thought that was against the rules."

"You want me to be honest?" I ask.

Sam folds his arms and nods. "Yep. All the way."

"Well, number one, I'm doing it because I said I would, and number two, she could be a platinum artist. You think I don't want to be on the ground floor of that?"

"Of course you do! You are Sunday 'Got My Mind on My Money' Tolliver!" Sam exclaims.

"You say that like it's a bad thing. What's wrong with me trying to get mine?"

Sam shrugs, like he always does when he doesn't want to answer my questions. "I think I've got a track that'll work for Bethany."

Sam presses a few buttons on his Yamaha keyboard and smooth-sounding music pours out of the speakers. It almost has a Latin feel with the hollow drumbeat and notes plucked on guitar strings instead of strummed.

"You did this?" I ask Sam. I'm totally impressed with his skills right now.

"Yeah, it's something I've been working on for a while. This new keyboard I got for graduation really has some nice effects."

"It's kind of big, though! Are you gonna bring it with you on campus at Georgia Tech?"

Sam shifts on his stool and strokes the keys on the keyboard. "I might not be going to Georgia Tech."

"For real? Well, where are you going?"

"Might not be going to college at all right now. Our music is really taking off, and I think it's about to blow up even further."

My eyes widen. Sam and I have talked about college so much that this surprises me. Or maybe I've done all the talking and he's only listened. It's kind of hazy to me now.

"I still want to go to college. It'll just be after I ride out this ten or fifteen minutes of fame."

"What makes you think we won't be in it longer than that?" I ask. "Look at Mystique and Zillionaire."

"They're like special cases, Sunday. We've got a good five years to make as much paper as we can. Then we'll just be regular, you know?"

I consider Sam's ideas about fame. I think that people who aren't really talented end up falling off the map after a few hit records. But this doesn't apply to Sam! He's a great keyboard player and producer. And he plays the cello too! I mean seriously, he's a real musician. Not just some dude with a beat machine.

"I still think you should go to college. Not just for our education! Think of the fraternity parties, step shows, and football games."

"I'll go to school in a few years."

Sam's track continues to loop in the background of our conversation. It plays so many times that it's all up in my head. I feel a hook forming around notes and drums.

I sing, "Say that you will. . . . I need to know that you're gonna be here. . . . Say what you won't do. . . . You won't hurt me . . . and I'll never lose you."

Sam beams a smile in my direction when I'm done. "How is it that you can write all these love songs, and you don't know anything about love?"

"You don't know what I know about!"

I'm offended that he would even say that to me. I'm even more irritated that he's right. But who says you have to know about love to write a love song? I know what I think love feels like, and I know I haven't felt anything close to what I'm imagining.

"Then tell me, Sunday. What do you know about love?" Sam's teasing voice makes me look at the tan berber carpet on the floor.

"Don't worry about what I know. You just keep the beats coming, and I'll keep writing the lyrics."

"That's all I am to you?" Sam asks. "A dude with nice tracks?"

"You know I don't feel that way, but I really don't want to talk about love, you know? It's too much trouble. Let's keep the conversation light."

"Gotcha! Sam and Sunday light!" Sam says in a tone that tells me he's a little bit irritated with me, but I'm irritated too, at the way he put our names together like that. Did he have to say, Sunday *and* Sam? It's almost like I'm talking to a brick wall with this dude!

I'm not trying to be wifed up! Dang!

Sam reaches out and flips the little bracelet on my wrist. It's the one he bought me, with the little *S* charm that dangles. He'd bought it for me when he was trying to be my boyfriend, and I wasn't ready. I wear the bracelet because it's cute, not because it means anything.

I finger the bracelet thoughtfully. "Do you want it back? If it bothers you for me to wear it, you know you can have it back, right?"

"I don't want it back. I gave it to you."

Now, we're staring at one another. I'm not sure where the conversation is supposed to go next. I guess it's my turn to speak.

"So . . . demo for Bethany. Three songs. We'll give her hot stuff, and see what happens from there. It'll be about selling it to Epsilon, I think, since they're the only record company where we have real connections."

"Bethany gets a record deal, and then what?"

I tap my chin until my thoughts become clear. "Then, we get paid to write the songs on her album, but this time we get royalties. No work-for-hire stuff like we did for Dreya."

"Don't get mad at the work for hire," Sam says. "It got us in the door."

When we wrote the songs for Dreya's album, we made an agreement with Epsilon Records that was like a deal with the devil. We don't get any money in royalties, no matter how many records Dreya sells, nor do we get any additional money from the song we did on Mystique's record.

"I'm not mad about it, but we already took one loss. I'm definitely not trying to take another one."

"Okay, so how are you going to explain it to Dreya?"

"I don't answer to her, and she's not my mother. I don't really care if she's angry or not, as long as I make money for my tuition. And that's for real."

"Okay, then. Let's do the dang thang!" Sam exclaims.

5

It's quiet in our house for a change. Mom and I both sit on opposite sides of the couch reading. Normally, the TV would be on or Manny would be somewhere crying for some juice. But right now . . . total quiet. This . . . right here . . . love it!

"How was your date, Mom?" I ask, breaking the silence.

Mom looks up from her book and smiles. It's not that faraway smile she gets on her face when she sees or talks about Carlos, but it's a smile nonetheless. She hasn't been smiling a lot lately, so this is a good thing.

"He was nice. Just another letter carrier named Jimmy. I've known him for years."

"Where'd y'all go?"

My mom laughs out loud. "You nosy!"

"I'm just trying to hold it down for my boy Carlos," I say.

This makes my mother's smile twist into an irritated frown. "Yeah. I tried to hold out for Carlos too, but I'm lonely. He doesn't even call on a regular basis."

"But Carlos loves you, Mom."

"Yeah, well, I've heard a few things that don't sit right about Carlos. I think we might be better off without him."

I kick both my feet out from under me, so I can stretch while I consider what my mother just laid on me. She's heard some things that didn't sit right about Carlos? This reminds me what Dilly said about Carlos not being on the up and up. Maybe he was telling the truth.

"What did you hear?" I ask.

"Nothing that I'm about to share with you, Sunday. You don't need to know about all that."

"I do need to know. That's how I end up in the middle of stuff. That stuff that went down in New York was crazy, Mom."

Mom nods sadly and stretches her legs out too. "It was crazy, and I wish that you hadn't been afraid to say something to me or at least Big D."

Why does everyone expect me to know the right thing to do because I'm smart? I don't know everything! And while everybody is looking at this with their twenty/twenty hindsight vision, wasn't none of them there with me thinking my mom and my little cousin could be hurt.

"I wish I had said something. Dilly hates me now."

Mom inhales and sighs. "Can you blame him, Sunday? Even though I can't stand his chicken-head sister and wannabe gangsta brother, he seems like a nice boy. He didn't deserve to be wrapped up in that either."

"I've tried to apologize to him, and he's not hearing it."

There's a long pause before my mother replies. "Give him some time, and then apologize again."

"And if he's still mad?" I ask.

"Do you care about being friends with him?" she asks.

I ponder this for a moment. I do like Dilly as a person, or I should say I *did* like him. Until the kidnapping attempt, he was funny and a blast to hang out with. Now, he just seems angry.

"I miss how he used to be. He was cool and talented," I finally say after I gather my thoughts.

"Do you care about being friends with him?" My mom repeats.

"Yes. I think so."

"Then you apologize again, and then again. Apologize until you're blue in the face, Sunday. You put that boy's life in danger, and I know you thought you were protecting me and Manny, but it doesn't change anything."

A knot forms in my throat, which tells me that I'm on the verge of tears. I don't usually get all emotional about stuff my mom says, but she's coming with some real tough love right now. I do need to make Dilly understand that I never meant for him to get hurt, and about how sorry I am.

"Don't cry about it, Sunday. Just fix it."

"That's easier said than done, Mom."

"You'd be surprised at what a sincere apology can do."

I spend a few minutes quietly reflecting on my mother's wisdom. It's not often that she drops knowledge on me, because I'm dang near the perfect kid. But when I do need it, my mama can bring it, know what I mean?

Then, like the hurricane that she is, Aunt Charlie bursts through the front door, wrecking our quiet flow.

"Sunday! You need to explain this right now!" Aunt Charlie screams at the top of her lungs while waving a *Variety* magazine in the air.

I lift an eyebrow, wondering what foolishness she's on now. "What are you talking about, Aunt Charlie?"

She pokes out her bony hip and flips to a page in the magazine. She flips the pages so hard that a few of them rip right out of the magazine and fall to the floor.

Aunt Charlie reads aloud, "Sunday Tolliver of Mystical Sounds just inked a deal with BET for a reality show based on the video shoot for her hit single, 'Can U See Me.' The show will also follow Ms. Tolliver during her first days as a college freshman at Spelman College. Thugged-out Truth and ghetto-fabulous cousin Drama take a backseat to Sunday, but all three can be seen on *Backstage: The Epsilon Summer Tour,* airing on BET nine p.m. on Thursdays this fall."

My mother bites her lip. Of course, she knows about the show. In fact, she's been bugging me to go ahead and tell Aunt Charlie to get it out of the way. But I've been stalling, because I knew this would happen.

"It sounds self-explanatory to me," my mother says as she turns the page in her book.

Aunt Charlie narrows her eyes and growls. "Shawn! You're just as bad. I know you had something to do with this. She wouldn't have signed this deal without talking to you about it."

Mom nods. "Yeah, I knew about it. So what?"

"So what? So *what*? Why wasn't Dreya a part of this, Sunday?"

I clear my throat, close my book, and place it on my lap. "BET wasn't interested in signing Dreya up for another season. The only reason she's going to be on the show at all is because I begged them to let her go to my video shoot in Barbados."

"But why didn't they want her back?" Aunt Charlie asks. "She has got to be more interesting than your little corny behind."

Now I feel myself getting extra heated, but I'm not about to disrespect my auntie. "I guess they thought corny was better than ghetto. They said I'm a more positive example for young people."

"Where's that Big D? I know he had something to do with this. He's been trying to push my baby to the background since y'all went on tour."

As I jump up from the couch, my book falls to the floor. "He has not! Dreya was the one on tour acting like some kind of diva from the hood! Plus, she didn't even graduate from high school!"

My mom interjects. "Charlie, I think you need to wait and see the reality show, before you question why they didn't want to fool with Dreya anymore."

"You've seen it?" I ask. I didn't know my mom was cool with Big D all like that.

"I didn't watch all of the episodes, but from what I did see, Dreya was acting a fool, Charlie. I mean, she acts like she doesn't even want this music career. She acts like this record deal is not a gift."

"A gift?" Aunt Charlie scoffs. "She's a gift to the record industry. Now y'all haters are trying to keep her down."

My mother and I both give Aunt Charlie blank stares. Then we look at each other and burst into laughter. This, of course, enrages Aunt Charlie even further. She throws the *Variety* magazine at my mother.

"You betta slow your roll, Charlie. I ain't playing with you."

I cover my mouth and giggle into my hand. I love when the big sister comes out, and my mother starts fussing at Aunt Charlie.

"Auntie, maybe if Dreya acts like she's got some sense when we go and do my video shoot, then they'll give her a show."

"You need to talk to her," my mom adds.

"My baby doesn't have to tone down who she is for anybody. And don't think she's gonna kiss your behind because of this video shoot."

"Nobody thinks that, Aunt Charlie."

Aunt Charlie's cell phone rings in her gigantic Baby Phat purse. "Dreya? . . . Where are you? . . . The emergency room! I'm gonna wring that little ropehead's neck."

My mother stands to her feet and pulls her shoes on. "Mom, what are you doing?" I ask.

"Didn't you hear your Aunt Charlie? Dreya's in the hospital."

Aunt Charlie holds the phone away from her face. "She said that she and Truth got into an argument and she fell running away from his car. Broke her ankle."

I roll my eyes. Why are Truth and Dreya dead set on becoming the next Whitney and Bobby?

"Are you coming, Sunday?" Aunt Charlie asks when she presses End on the cell phone.

"No. I've got something else I need to do."

I think my mom and auntie are capable of taking care of Dreya's goofy self and her unnecessary drama. Seeing her with a cast on her ankle because of an argument with Truth wouldn't make me feel anything close to sympathetic for her.

"Well, what are you about to do?" my mom asks.

"I'm going to talk to Dilly. I'm taking your advice."

My mom beams a bright smile over in my direction. "Good. Real friends are worth it."

"Dilly ain't her friend," Aunt Charlie says. "He's just another groupie squirrel trying to get a nut and a record deal."

My mom shakes her head and says to Aunt Charlie, "That's why I'm your only friend."

6

I'm on a mission.

Sitting in front of Dilly's house in my car, trying to decide whether or not I want to go up and knock on the door. I guess I could've called or sent Dilly a text first, but since he's in trip-out mode and ain't even trying to talk to me, I don't even know if that would be the best thing.

My phone rings, and it's Dilly! "Hey."

"Why are you in front of my house?" Dilly asks with attitude.

I expected to be able to work my nerve up before I got the apology out, but it doesn't seem like Dilly's gonna give me the time, space, or opportunity.

"I just want to talk to you, Dilly, without anyone else around. Just us."

Silence.

"Dilly, you there?" I ask. I know he's still there—I can

hear his heavy and ragged breathing. He sounds like he's got a cold or something.

"I'm here. What do you want to talk about?"

I don't want to do this over the phone! "Dilly, can you come outside? I'd rather see your face when I'm talking to you."

"You don't get to make the rules, Sunday. The last time I trusted you, I almost wound up dead, remember?"

No, he did not just hang up on me! Okay . . .

I get out of my car, even though I sooo don't want to walk up to the front door of LaKeisha's crib. This is walking smack dab in the middle of enemy territory.

Their porch is kinda raggedy with rotted-out floor-boards, and a ratty old welcome mat. I ring the doorbell, hoping and praying that Dilly is home alone and I don't have to talk to LaKeisha or Bryce.

The door flies open and LaKeisha is standing her ghetto butt in front of me looking like a bowl of Froot Loops with her rainbow-colored hair weave. She looks me up and down with a stank look on her face. I stand my ground, though, and gave her a stank look right back.

"I know you ain't ringing on my doorbell when you tried to get my brother killed. You need to roll up out of here real quick," LaKeisha says.

"Can you tell Dilly I'm out here?" I ask. So not trying to hear all her noise.

"Oh, you real bold. You ain't scared I'm gonna knock you on your behind?"

I let out a soft chuckle. "Naw, I'm really not. 'Cause I

know you want your brother to get a record deal so you can upgrade from that synthetic weave."

"You can't stop my brother from blowing up."

I shrug. "You wanna see how quickly Epsilon and Zillionaire drop him once I say the word?"

"You think you all that?" LaKeisha asks.

"Naw, but maybe you need to ask Mystique if I'm all that."

LaKeisha narrows her eyes and clucks her tongue one time. I knew mentioning Mystique, Zillionaire, and Epsilon Records would make the difference. I don't care how much they want to make me a part of the drama between Bryce and Carlos, bottom line is they want Dilly to blow up and make their world a better place.

Finally, after looking me up and down once more, LaKeisha says, "Make it quick. Dilly ain't trying to talk to you no way."

I'm assuming that LaKeisha is done trying to intimidate me because she turns her back and walks away. I chuckle as I watch the fake Baby Phat logo fall off the back of her knockoff jeans. Raggedy, skanked-out heifer.

It takes a few moments for Dilly to come to the door. His arms are crossed like he's not ready to talk this thing through.

I wait for him to step outside and close the door before I begin. At least he can tell that I don't want to have this conversation with him and LaKeisha's nosy butt, since she is sure to be listening near the door.

"I've got to go to the studio soon, Sunday, so what's up?" Dilly asks in a much less hostile tone than he had on the telephone.

"I just want to apologize, Dilly. No excuses. I should've let somebody know what was going down, and I didn't."

Dilly gives me silence. His arms are still crossed as he leans back on the front door. It's a little bit more relaxed, but not exactly friendly.

I pull on the top of my ponytail, trying to make my brain think of something else to say. I didn't really plan this speech. I'm sort of freestyling this.

I continue with a question. "Do you think you can get past this?"

"Can you get past your beef with my family?" Dilly's response is immediate, like this question was already on the tip of his tongue.

"If I couldn't get over my beef with your family, I wouldn't be here right now."

Dilly takes off his baseball cap and runs a hand over his deep waves. Arms not crossed anymore. This is a good sign.

"Sunday, I want us to be cool, because I really like Bethany, and she says y'all are really tight."

I choose not to comment on the friendship situation with me and Bethany. We used to be best friends, but to call us close right now is a stretch. She's engaged in too much grimy behavior for me to say we're tight.

"I want us to be cool too," I reply. "But not because of Bethany. I think you're really talented, and I like having you in my camp."

"Your camp?" A smile creeps onto Dilly's face.

"Yeah, my camp. It's gonna be my reality show and my video shoot in Barbados."

"It's all about Sunday right now, huh?" Dilly asks. I don't think I like the sarcastic, hateriffic tone in his voice.

"No . . . but the reality show is gonna be based on the video shoot. It'll be fun. You're fun. And I think we should all be there. We deserve it after all the drama from the summer tour."

"I'm down," Dilly says.

"Yeah, well, I'm gonna need you to act just a little bit more friendly toward me if this is gonna work."

Finally, a real smile from Dilly. "I can do that. As long as you aren't unleashing your goons on me again."

"My goons? I didn't have anything to do with those dudes. Seriously."

I can't help but think of the check for twenty-five thousand dollars. I put it in my college bank account and it hasn't bounced yet, so I'm pretty sure it's the real deal. I just wonder where it came from. It could've been from Los Diablos, Carlos's cousin's gang. If it is from them, I don't think I even want it.

Dilly's phone buzzes and he reads the screen. "Are we done?" he asks. "Bethany's gonna be here soon, and we're going to Zillionaire's crib to work on a cut for his next album."

"Zac's doing another album? I thought he was about to release one of his artists."

"Nah. He's going to kind of debut us on his album. Let us do a verse on a few songs. I've almost got him convinced to let Bethany sing a hook."

One of my eyebrows shoots up involuntarily. I think it's my money eyebrow. You know how some people's hands itch when they're about to get money? Well, my eyebrow gets really twitchy.

"Really? Well, I better get busy on those songs for her then."

Dilly clears his throat. "Bethany told me why you're doing this for her. And I don't think you should do it if you don't want to."

I can't believe Bethany would tell Dilly about that craziness with Truth. "What did she tell you exactly?"

Dilly replies, "She said that you caught her making out with Truth, and that she said she wouldn't hook up with him if you'd help her with her album."

Wow! She actually told him the real deal! I'm beyond shocked. Maybe she really is trying to be a better person. I hope so for Dilly's sake.

"And you think I shouldn't help her now?"

"Well, I know she's not gonna mess with Truth regardless. And since the cat is out of the bag anyway, I don't really see the point. I mean, Dreya knows about them hooking up now."

"What if I told you that I think Bethany could be a star?"

"You think so?"

I nod. "She wants it badly enough. Worse than me and Dreya combined. So, yeah, I think she could do it. Sam and I are working on some really hot stuff for her."

"And Dreya won't be mad about you helping her?"

"Heck yeah, Dreya's gonna be mad. But at this point in the game, I can't worry about what's going to make her mad. It's about the paper and the grind, you know?"

"The paper and the grind," Dilly repeats my mantra.

I hold my arms out to Dilly, hoping that he doesn't leave me hanging and lets me have a hug. For a long moment he just stares at me like he hasn't made up his mind.

I drop my arms. "Okay, maybe we're not ready for hugs yet. How about a fist bump?"

Dilly grins and balls his fist. He bumps it with mine, but at the end he gives me an awkward one-arm hug. LaKeisha peeks through the curtains with a scowl on her face.

"I guess I should go inside," Dilly says. "I need to roll out in a few."

"All right then. See you at Big D's or wherever."

"Okay."

I jog back to my car, not wanting to give LaKeisha the chance to add any closing remarks. Don't need her ruining this moment for me and Dilly.

I feel a total weight lifted from me. Apologizing and getting forgiven are totally underrated. As much as my mom has been getting on my nerves lately (especially with the college-fund caper), I'm so glad I listened to her on this one.

Mission accomplished!

7

"We love you, Mystique!"

Having lunch with Mystique is the opposite of fun. It's more like having a root canal. And she always picks these spots where the Atlanta paparazzi are going to take her picture and the screaming fans are going to do what they do. Scream.

Mystique flings her fire-engine-red weave back and flashes an award-winning smile. "I love you too! I love you more!"

Then she turns her attention back to me. I stuff a forkful of salad into my mouth so that she can't see my sarcastic smirk. Sidebar, this salad is disgusting. Baby spinach, tomatoes, mushrooms, and carrots drizzled with olive oil and lemon.

One-hundred-percent healthy, zero-percent yummy.

"How is your salad?" Mystique asks.

I give her a blank stare. She already knows what it is.

"I know it doesn't taste that great, but it is really good for you, Sunday. All that junk you put into your body is horrible for you."

Shhhh! Can you hear that? It's my stomach growling for a slice of pepperoni pizza.

"I hear what you're saying, Mystique, but do you eat rabbit food all day, every day?"

She nods. "When I'm working I do. You'll learn that if you don't eat healthy while you're on the road, you'll get sick really easily."

I guess eating like this is all part of the game. Yeah, that doesn't make me feel any better.

"Speaking of going on the road," Mystique continues, "have you decided if your cousin and all of her foolishness are going with us to Barbados for your video shoot?"

I feel my eyebrows come together in a tightly knit frown. In the background a flash from one of the cameras nearly blinds me. Great. Now they're going to have a picture for the Internet bloggers of me mean mugging Mystique. All bad.

"I thought we had already decided that everyone was coming. Not just Dreya, but Truth, Bethany, Dilly, Sam, Big D, and Shelly too."

Mystique grins at me, and I'm not even sure I can decipher what it means. Has it *not* been decided?

"Well, it's really up to you, Sunday," Mystique says. "If you want them there on the island, ruining your vibe, that's totally up to you, but it's not like we need them for the reality show or the video."

I look down at my salad and spread the meager leaves

around on the plate. Why do I have to be the one to decide to cut my cousin loose? If Epsilon Records doesn't
want her around, all they have to do is say the word.
Why does it have to be about me betraying my own?

"If it's my decision, then they stay."

"You really want them to come?" Mystique asks. "Are
you doing this out of loyalty? Because this is not a loyal
business. Drama would've dropped you in a minute."

"First of all, I don't believe that. I know my cousin."

Mystique interrupts, "Really? What if I told you that
she tried to stop your record deal from happening? She
threatened to not record for Epsilon Records if they let
you sign to my label."

"I would say that I don't let other people's actions de-
fine my actions."

Mystique looks really frustrated right now. She takes
in a sharp breath and then takes several quick sips from
her water glass.

"Okay, fine," Mystique says. "They can go, but when
Drama and Bethany get to fighting like two alley cats,
don't say I didn't warn you."

"Dreya knows this is about her career, and she's not
going to let Bethany cost her a record deal."

"About Bethany and record deals—what's this I hear
about you writing songs for her demo?"

Mystique is getting a little bit overwhelming with all
these questions. She's up here interrogating me like she
gave birth to me. I've got one mother, and she does *not*
wear a bright red weave.

"How do you even know we're working on music for
Bethany? It's not like we're advertising it."

"Dilly told Zac, and Zac told me."

Without thinking, I roll my eyes. This little chain of gossip is too dang intimate. I can't sneeze without someone reporting it back to Mystique. Is it really all that serious? I mean, dang!

"Yeah, I'm working on music for Bethany. It's a side project."

Mystique clears her throat and sips some more of her water. "I'm not sure you have time for side projects right now. I think you need to focus on Sunday and Sunday Tolliver only."

Okay, I'm tripping right now because this is the chick who's got a million side projects going on. She sings, she's a songwriter, and she's got a record label, fashion line, and a whole bunch of other stuff. She's even going to try her hand at acting.

So why do I have to focus on one thing?

"Seems like you do a good job of multitasking," I say. "I'm just trying to be like you."

Mystique beams and the cameras flash again. I wonder what this caption will read. It certainly won't be what's running through my head. *Mystique's protégée restrains herself from jumping across the table to snatch off Mystique's weave.*

"I'm flattered that you want to be like me, but you aren't there yet, honey. The first thing I did was make Mystique a brand name. You can't truly bring anyone else up until you get yours and the competition is no longer a threat."

Now, I'm the one sipping water. "Bethany is talented

too. She's been a part of my group for years, and she could make me a lot of money on the back end of things."

I think that Mystique doesn't understand who I am. I don't want to be an internationally known performer who can't even walk down the street without being photographed. I'm content to fade into obscurity, while cashing songwriting checks for the artists. Give me rich without the fame, all day every day.

"My brand name," I say, "is Sunday Tolliver the songwriter. Hello! Do you know me? I'm about to go to Spelman in the fall!"

"I've heard Bethany sing. I think she would be competition for you, and I don't think you need to be doing any songwriting favors for your competition. It is a favor, right?" Mystique asks.

"No . . . well . . . it started out as me helping her because I wanted her to leave Truth alone. She was only messing with him because he promised to help her get a record deal."

Mystique laughs out loud. "I'm sorry, Sunday, but that sounds really stupid. You're going to *help* Bethany to keep her from hooking up with Truth? Why do you even care?"

Where has this chick been for the past forty-five minutes? How is she not getting the point? I hold it down for mine. All day, every day.

"I care, because Truth is my cousin's boyfriend. I don't want her hurt. What's not to understand?"

Mystique shakes her head, the look of frustration back on her face. "Well, are you at least getting paid for this foolishness?"

"Bethany doesn't have any money. I'll get paid on the back end."

"If you're not getting paid on the front end, then it's a favor. I'd drop her like it's hot, if I were you."

Mystique's unwanted advice session is interrupted by her cell phone ringing. It's comical seeing Mystique dig around in that gigantic purse looking for her BlackBerry. She almost misses her call every time.

"Hey babe!" She catches it in time. "Yeah, me and Sunday are having lunch. . . . We're talking about her destiny and her journey. . . . Yeah. . . . Everything that's going to happen for her once she gets rid of all this dead weight."

She looks at me, and all I'm thinking is, *Wow . . . okay. . . .*

Mystique continues, "Oh, I forgot to tell her about that! I'll tell her now. . . . All right, baby. . . . See you later. . . . Bye!"

"You forgot to tell me what?" I ask as soon as she presses End on her phone.

"Well . . . I just wanted to ask if you and Sam are dating. Are y'all official?"

Okay, I have to pause before I answer this. Because this does not feel okay. Not the impish grin on her face, nor the fact that she and Zac are plotting behind my back and keeping secrets. I'm not amused.

"No. Me and Sam are not dating officially. We had one official date since the tour, but I don't think that counts as officially dating. So, I'm going to have to say my answer is no."

"Well, good, because we have a wonderful idea that we think will really put you and Dilly on the map."

I lift an eyebrow at Mystique. "What is it? A collaboration?"

"Something like that. The BET producers thought that you and Dilly had really great chemistry, especially in the prom scene where he was freestyling to you."

"And?"

"And . . . they think you should play that up in the next installment of your reality show. They think your fans would like to see a fun yet squeaky-clean romance for you on the air."

"No, no, and let me think really hard . . . NO!"

"Sunday, please don't say no yet. This is how it works in the industry. You don't have to kiss him or anything like that."

"Oh, I don't? Thank you, Mystique, for telling me what I don't have to do with my own lips!" Is she out of her mind?

"Shhh!! Don't make a scene, Sunday. You never know who's got a mini-cam."

"At this point, I don't care."

"Look, just play up the fact that the viewers will think you two like each other. It will blow your career off the map. Trust me on this one."

"Okay, are you forgetting that Dilly basically hates me right now? We're just getting back to speaking terms, and now you want us to have an on-screen romance?"

"Zac is gonna talk to Dilly, and we think we can convince him that this is the best thing for his career. He really wants his record to come out, so we think he'll be all for it."

I shake my head trying to erase the craziness she's spewing. "Okay, so what am I supposed to tell Sam?"

"You don't have to tell him anything. You just said he's not your boyfriend."

Big ol' sigh. "Yeah, he's not my boyfriend, but I still care about him."

"I don't know, Sunday. If you must tell him, I'm sure you'll figure something out."

A lot of help she is! She just laid this whammy on me and is gonna make me deal with the fallout. The last time we tried to have a fake love triangle with Truth, me, and Sam, it was all bad.

Plus, Sam just told me that I keep playing games. If I agree to do this, he just might be right. Because if this isn't a game, I don't know what is.

8

When I get home after my lunch with Mystique, I'm
still spinning a little bit trying to figure out how I'm
going to tell Sam about this new idea of Zac and Mystique's. Because, yeah, I'm definitely going to tell him. He
might not be my boyfriend, but I feel like I owe this to
him. I don't need to learn another lesson on how keeping
secrets can hurt. Been there, done that, bought the T-shirt,
returned it with the tags still on.

There's a car parked in front of our house that I don't
recognize. And I am so not in the mood for another surprise this afternoon.

I walk into the house, all the while bracing myself for
craziness. Truth is here, and there's a woman with him
who I don't know. She's definitely older than me, but not
as old as my mom or Aunt Charlie. She's got long braids
that come to the middle of her back. Her bare arms sport
many tattoos. There are a few names, a cross, two cher-

ries, some sort of bird and a tiger. I can see that she has absolutely no theme going on with her tattoo game.

Sidebar—Aunt Charlie is mean mugging both the lady and Truth.

What immediately strikes me is the expression on Truth's face. I've never seen him look so contrite. But if I was him, I'd back up a few paces from Aunt Charlie. She's furious about Dreya's broken ankle, and she's looking like she wants to return the favor.

"Do what I said, Truth! Tell them," the woman says.

"All right, Ma. Dag!"

Okay . . . wow! This is Truth's mama! I can see the apple didn't fall too far from the ghetto tree. I wonder if they have an Apple Bottoms tree in their yard? SMH! I'm laughing quietly inside!

This looks like it's going to be interesting, so I pull up a seat next to Manny. He obviously thinks it's movie time or something, because little dude has apple juice in his favorite sippy cup and a bowl of popcorn in his lap.

Manny says, "Hey, Sunday. What's up, cuzzo?"

"Hey, Little Manny. What's going on?"

He sucks his teeth. "This fool up here trying to apologize to my mama for putting his hands on my sister."

Truth cuts his eyes at Manny, and Manny slams his bowl of popcorn down like he's the man up in here. "What? You gone break my ankle too?" Manny asks.

My mother gives Manny a look that says, *Boy, you better be quiet before you get a whuppin'*. But I don't see why he has to be quiet! He lives here!

"Tell her, Truth!" his mother says again, this time sounding more impatient than the first time.

"Um, my mother didn't raise me to put my hands on women. I'm sorry about what I did to Dreya. Even though she started it and put her hands on me first, this is not the way I was raised, and I'm so sorry."

Aunt Charlie says nothing, but she gives Truth a cold glare. I guess she's not buying it. My mother decides to step in.

She says, "We didn't raise Dreya to put her hands on a man or anybody else. So we're also disappointed in her, just like we're disappointed in you."

"Yes, ma'am," Truth says.

"Maybe y'all don't need to see one another anymore," my mother continues, "if y'all can't keep your hands off of one another. We don't want to see things escalate or for anyone to get seriously injured. You or Dreya."

"Yes, ma'am."

"Y'all both coming into your own with the music. So we think it's best if y'all put the relationship on hold indefinitely."

"But, ma'am, I really do love Dreya."

"If you love her," my mom says, "you will have enough sense to get yourself some help and be mature the next time you try to be her boyfriend."

"Yeah, it's on hold for good," Aunt Charlie says. "You better be glad my sister is here and she won't let me give you some of the same medicine you gave my daughter."

"No, Charlie. Violence is not the answer," my mother replies. "Putting your hands on him is not the answer. That's what got us to where we are now—violence. That's not where we need to be right now. We need to get y'all

to a place where y'all can be prosperous like God is calling you to be."

Uh-oh. My mom done brought God into the conversation. She's about to lay hands on him and pray. I know it.

"Come here, let me pray for you, boy," my mom says.
I knew it!

Aw, man. You don't mess with my mama and her praying! Oh my goodness. Truth is fixing to catch the Holy
Ghost up in here.

My mother lays her hands on Truth's head and says a
prayer for him. She whispers in his ear so that we can't
hear what she's saying. And do you know this wannabe
thug breaks down crying?

Wait a minute. Dude is like for-real crying . . . boo-hoo
crying on my mother's shoulder. And she's hugging him
like he's never gotten a hug in his entire life. I actually
kind of think that might be true, because his mother is
looking super uncomfortable right now. Maybe she's
never given him the love that he needs.

"Truth, whenever you get the urge to put your hands
on someone, I want you to remember the words I just
prayed for you," my mother says.

"Yes, ma'am."

"And Truth, remember, I love you, your mother loves
you, and above all Jesus loves you. I believe you have a
good heart and I believe you can change."

"I don't believe it. If he puts his hand on you once,
he'll do it again."

My mother narrows her eyes into little slits in Aunt
Charlie's direction. "Most of the time, that is true, but I
do believe that God can change anybody who wants it.

Truth, baby, just let God work on your heart and take all that anger away. You just gotta give it to Him."

"All right, Ms. Tolliver. I'ma do that."

"Okay, baby."

My mother gives Truth's mother a hug too. Maybe because she's standing there with tears in her eyes, and my mom just kind of knows when people need a hug.

I think she needs to turn around and hug Aunt Charlie too, because she's still mean mugging Truth.

"Stay away from my daughter," Aunt Charlie says as Truth and his mother leave the house. "Stay away. From. My. Daughter."

9

My nose crinkles into an irritated frown as Mystique holds up a two-piece bathing suit from her mother, Ms. Layla's, summer collection. This thing is extra teeny. It looks like three Doritos held together with dental floss. I don't like, and my mama definitely won't like. Voting no.

Dreya is here with me, supposedly for moral support, and because I trust her taste in clothes. Although we have different styles, she knows what I like, and will quickly veto something that looks insane. But I also asked her to come because she's been in her apartment sulking ever since Truth broke up with her.

Getting Dreya out of the apartment didn't stop the sulking, though. She sits slumped in a chair with her air cast extended and crutches on the floor next to her.

"You don't think this is cute?" Mystique asks.

"Maybe if I could see it, I'd think it was cute. I don't

think I'd be comfortable with my behind hanging out, and it most definitely will be in that suit."

Ms. Layla tosses her head back and cackles. For some reason, she sounds like the Joker off of the Batman movies. It scares me.

"You should be happy your body is so beautiful," Ms. Layla says when her laughing is done. "You won't have that wonderful figure for long."

"I like my figure," I say. "I just don't want to show it to the entire world in my video. How about this?" I hold up a much more modest white tankini.

Dreya bursts into laughter. "Girl, stop. That looks like a chubby-girl suit. You cannot wear that in your video."

"I did design that for girls with a little thicker physique than you," Ms. Layla explains.

Mystique grabs another bikini from the rack. This one has more material, but it's still hot. It's pleather, and the top is a halter with a zipper. The bottom is boy shorts. Hotness!

"Does this work for you?" Mystique asks.

"Yes. I likes. But why does it have to be white? I look good in gold or turquoise."

"That's the theme of the video. You're going to be in all white in every scene. And Dilly will be in different colors until the last scene, when he's going to wear white too."

"Dilly is the love interest in Sunday's video?" Dreya asks. "Wow, you're really trying to make Sam mad."

"If he gets mad about a video shoot," Mystique snaps, "then he's not the boy for her. She's going to have lots of shoots with lots of hot guys."

Dreya chuckles. "I wouldn't exactly describe Dilly as a hot guy."

I think about this for a moment. Even though I'm not digging Dilly in a crush kind of way, his hotness is undeniable. Especially when he starts rapping. He's got that pretty-boy steez on lock.

"He's not hot to you," I say. "But I think a lot of girls will crush on Dilly when his album finally comes out."

Mystique says, "That's exactly why I think you should play up the love-interest thing on the reality show! That will be hot."

I clear my throat and say, "Listen, Mystique, about the whole love-interest thing. I think it'll be better for me to just be real. I don't have a boyfriend, because I'm getting my grind on, and I don't think there's anything wrong with that."

"There's nothing wrong with that," Mystique agrees. "But I'm trying to help you sell records."

"Why can't I sell them by being myself? Plus, Sam might not be my boyfriend, but he is my really good friend."

Dreya interjects, "And you like him too! Stop trying to act all hard, Sunday. You like him."

Wow! Dreya gets on my nerves, but I feel a little smile on my lips. Of course, she's right, whether I admit it to Sam or not.

"Okay, Sunday. Don't play up the crush thing with Dilly. Epsilon Records will be disappointed, but I think I can convince them that you're doing it for a good reason," Mystique says.

"I don't know how that was gonna work anyway," Dreya says. "Dilly is dating that backstabbing Bethany."

Mystique nods. "Yes, I was going to try to get him to put that on pause for the show. But he and Bethany are talking about doing a song together."

Dreya lets out a snort. "She's is such a jock rider. She just couldn't let me and Sunday be successful without trying to latch on. I can't stand her."

Okay, I want to change the subject, because I haven't exactly broken it to Dreya that I'm working on Bethany's music. I try to communicate to Mystique with my eyes that we should ixnay the Bethany conversation, but she's still talking. . . .

"Actually, she's got a nice song. I heard one of the tracks that Sunday did and it was hot. She's got a raspy, soulful sound. You don't expect it coming from her! It's like you look at her and think you're gonna get a Taylor Swift sound, and it's more Alicia Keys."

Dreya narrows her eyes at me. "Sunday . . . for real? Why?"

How can I even explain this now in a way that makes sense? For me to tell Dreya the truth, I'll have to admit that I knew Bethany was messing around with Truth on the tour. And that, I think, will be an even bigger betrayal.

"She asked. . . . I said yes. End of story," I say curtly.

Ms. Layla interrupts any additional commentary by Dreya by showing me two white sundresses—both long.

"I think I'd like to see you in one of these at the end of the video," Ms. Layla says. "You can wear your hair in a pretty spiral curl updo, with minimal makeup. You'll be gorgeous."

I nod. "I'd wear either of these dresses."

Dreya says, "So, I'm trying to figure out how you came to be writing songs for Bethany behind my back. It's not like y'all are friends, since she dated your ex-boyfriend."

"Give it a rest!" I reply. "It doesn't matter how it came about. Even if me and Bethany aren't really all that close anymore, we came up together, and the least I could do is write her a song or two."

Mystique laughs out loud. "You girls kill me with these loyalty rules! Why does it matter if you came up together? What does that have to do with anything?"

"It means a lot," Dreya says. "Don't you have any home girls from back in the day? Wait . . . do you have any girlfriends at all? I only see you in the tabloids with your mama or Zillionaire."

"They're all I need. Girlfriends get in the way. Most of them were always jealous and hated on my success. Had to cut all of the haters loose."

Dreya and I exchange glances. I don't know what Dreya's thinking, but I'm feeling like Mystique doesn't really believe her own hype. She sounds kind of sad about not having any friends besides her mother and fiancé.

Big D pulls up in front of Ms. Layla's boutique so abruptly that his tires squeal as he hits the brakes. He jumps out of the car and jogs inside.

"What's going on, Darius?" Ms. Layla asks. "You drove up like a bank robber leaving the scene of the crime."

Big D takes big gulps of air, as he tries to catch his breath. "I need to talk to Sunday. Outside."

Now I'm alarmed. "What's up? Why can't you just say it in front of everybody?"

"I can't." Big D shakes his head. "It won't take long, baby girl. I promise."

I've never seen Big D look this twisted about anything. "All right."

I follow Big D out of Ms. Layla's boutique. His body language is weird and nervous. He presses a button to unlock his SUV.

"Hop in, Sunday."

I get in on the passenger side, while Big D gets in on his side. He slumps in his seat a little. It's such a small movement that if I hadn't been paying attention, I wouldn't have seen it. But it was a slump, and it looked weary.

"What in the world is going on, Big D? You look twisted, for real."

"Your father came to see me."

I can feel my face going into contortions. My father? The man I haven't seen since my seventh-grade promotion ceremony? What in the world? How does he even know Big D? He doesn't even know me really, but he knows my producer? Get the heck out of here.

"My father? You talking about my biological father?"

Big D nods. "Yeah, Jonah Christopher, your biological. He says that he needs to be in on the decision making for your career."

"Is he crazy? There's no way he's going to have anything to do with my career! How do you even know him?"

"That's the thing. I don't know him. He knows Bryce and LaKeisha. He was in business with them on some things."

"What kinds of things?" I ask, already knowing the answer is something illegal.

My father has been in and out of jail since I was born. I guess my mom just has a thing for men with that thug quality to them. Not me, though. I see my mother every day, by herself and lonely because of dealing with these dudes. My daddy and Carlos. Although, Carlos was supposed to be different. He was supposed to take care of my mom and me. Now he's gone too.

"They've got some real-estate thing going, where they buy foreclosed houses at a huge discount, and then resell them or rent them out. Then they take out a loan against the equity in the house and use the money for other investments."

"Is it on the up and up?" I ask.

Big D shrugs and then drums his fingers on the steering wheel like he's stalling for an answer. "They haven't been arrested yet."

"No arrests have been made. Wow. Did you tell him to kick rocks?"

"Sunday . . . I told him I'd set up a meeting with the two of you. He really wants to see you."

"Why would you do that, Big D? You could've asked me first."

"You don't exactly say no when the person asking is carrying a gun."

My eyes stretch wide open in surprise. "Did he threaten you? OMG. I don't believe this."

"He didn't exactly threaten me. He just made it clear that he intended to meet with you whether I wanted it or not."

"This dude owes my mother thousands of dollars in back child support! He can't be a part of my career. My mom is gonna freak out when she hears this."

"Maybe you shouldn't tell her," Big D says.

"Man, stop playing. I don't keep important secrets anymore, remember? That was the agreement. I tell my mom anytime anything crazy is popping off."

"I wouldn't necessarily classify this as crazy."

Let's see. My dad, who I haven't seen in more than five years, pops up and wants to manage my career. AND he's kicking it with Bryce and LaKeisha, the ones responsible for my mother's boyfriend getting shot.

No. That's not crazy. It's not crazy at all.

Blank. Stare.

10

"**M**om, I've got something to tell you, and I think you should sit down."

My mother looks at me with narrowed eyes, and puts her hand on her hip. "Sunday, don't play games with me. What's going on? Are you pregnant?"

"What! Where did that come from? Mom, for real. This is important, and no, I'm not pregnant. I don't have a boyfriend and I'm not having sex."

My mother still gives me a suspicious stare-down as she sits on the couch in our living room. I had to wait all day until Aunt Charlie and Manny decided to go to the grocery store. It's always funny when Aunt Charlie comes home from the grocery store. She shops like a two-year-old. There's usually hot dogs, bologna, bread, cereal, milk, and soda. That's all. Not a vegetable in sight. As a matter of fact, I don't think Manny would know what a fruit or a vegetable was if he wasn't living over here with us.

I know, total sidebar. But I'm stalling here. Don't really know how to tell my mother about my dad showing up. I don't know how she's gonna take it.

"Well, what's going on, Sunday? I've got laundry to finish up, girl! And then I'm going to the movies with your aunt this evening."

"Who is keeping Manny? I've got to go to the studio for a meeting."

"He's going to have a sleepover with his big sister. A meeting about what?"

I unleash a big sigh. "That's what I've been trying to tell you."

"Okay, I'm sorry. Go ahead."

"My father wants to manage my career."

There. I got it out. As crazy as it sounds, I've said it. And now, I'm watching my mother's face contort into some sort of zombie face.

"Your daddy? You talked to your daddy?"

I shake my head. "He went to Big D, and told him he wants to be a part of the decision-making team on my career."

"I don't believe this. How did Jonah even know to contact Big D?"

"It has something to do with Bryce and LaKeisha. He's in some kind of business with them, I guess."

My mom lets out a long sigh. "Yeah, I heard he was fooling with them the last time he got out of jail. I was just hoping that he wouldn't come around us."

"Wait. You were hoping he wouldn't come around? I mean, I know you don't like him, but I haven't seen him in a long time. Shoot, pretty soon I'm gonna forget what he looks like."

"Sunday . . . your daddy . . . girl . . . you know I've never talked bad to you about your daddy."

"No, you never have, but I know he goes back and forth to jail. That can't be good."

"He did one good thing for me," my mother says. "He gave me you. I should've known he was gonna show up once your music career took off."

"What should I tell him?"

"Baby, I know you're used to me having all the answers, but I don't know what to say on this one. It's your decision."

I swallow hard. "But do you think I should let him help with my career?"

Long, long pause from my mom. I know that she doesn't like to say anything bad about my father to me. I get that. She doesn't want me to be jaded about men and all that. But I need her to help me on this one.

"I haven't seen your father for a long time, Sunday. Maybe he's changed. I don't know. You judge for yourself after you talk to him."

"Why does this all have to be happening right before my trip to Barbados? If this doesn't turn out right, it might ruin my trip."

She says, "I know, honey. But you leave for Barbados in a couple of days, so maybe it will go well and you won't have anything to worry about."

"That's all you're gonna say, Mom?"

"That's all I've got, Sunday. You let me know what you think, okay? We'll talk about it later."

My mom gets up from the couch, walks over to me, and gives me a big hug. I know she's got my back in this, even if she won't give her opinion.

I guess this is just something I've got to do on my own.

11

So I agreed to meet my father at the studio, although I couldn't bring myself to call him and set it up. He'd left his cell phone number with Big D, but I just couldn't call. I thought that if I heard his voice on the phone that I'd probably change my mind about the meeting. I had Big D call and set everything up.

My mom's words keep ringing in my head. *Maybe he's changed.*

What if he has changed? That would be great, but I don't know if that means I should let him be a part of my career. I'm thinking he's gonna have to work his way back up to that status. And what if he doesn't show up? I don't know how I would feel about that.

Shelly's going to cook us some dinner, and she and Big D are going to be close by, but in another room, in case I need them.

Big D sits down next to me on the leather couch in the

TV room. "You sure you want to do this alone? Maybe your mother should be here with you."

"Nah, she didn't want to come. She wanted me to make up my own mind."

"You seem nervous, Sunday. You're playing with your hands, biting your nails. Chill a little bit."

"You're the one who's got me nervous!"

"Okay. My bad. I just know that some things have popped off, and with Carlos getting shot and all, I don't know what to believe."

"You think my dad had something to do with that?"

"I don't know. Maybe," Big D says. "That's the word on the street."

Now that's just great. I'm about to see my dad for the first time in over five years and Big D drops this bomb on me. So not fair.

"You know what? I'm not gonna let anything about my mom and dad's relationship get in this conversation. Just because they've got bad blood between them, that doesn't have anything to do with me."

"Okay . . ."

"And I choose to believe that he didn't have anything to do with Carlos getting shot until I learn differently."

"I feel you on that, baby girl," Big D says. "Are you ready for Barbados? You got your passport and everything together?"

A little chuckle escapes from my mouth. "It's a little late in the day to be checking to see if I have my papers. We leave the day after tomorrow."

"I know. I'm just making small talk. Trying to keep you company until your dad gets here."

"Thanks, Big D. I appreciate you for that."

The doorbell rings, and curiously enough I'm caught off guard. I knew that my father was coming, but I still jumped when the doorbell sounded. Is that an omen or what?

"Well . . . me and Shelly will be upstairs chilling. Just holla if you need me."

"All right."

The doorbell rings again, so I go to the door to answer it. I can feel my feet dragging along, as if I don't want to see my dad. Maybe I'm afraid that after I tell him he's not going to be in charge of my career, he won't come back ever again.

This might be the last time I see him.

I open the door slowly, holding my breath the whole time. My father is standing there in jeans and a Phat Farm polo, looking almost exactly the same as the last time I saw him, with the exception of a few gray hairs in his goatee.

He holds his arms out for a hug, and my response is awkward at best. I kind of tumble into his arms in an unsure motion. He even smells the same. He still wears the same perfume my mom used to buy him for his birthday. Cool Water for Men.

"Sunday . . . wow. . . . You're . . . you're grown."

I blush and look at my feet. I am grown! I don't even know how to respond to this.

"Do you want to come in?"

I show my father to the leather couch and we both sit down.

"Big D is doing all right, ain't he?" my father says as he looks around at all of Big D's high-tech gadgets.

"I guess. He works really hard for his artists and gets them good opportunities."

"*His* artists? He doesn't own you."

I see he's gonna get directly to the point. He's not even gonna ask me about the last five years of my life? How about a "sorry I haven't been around"?

"Nobody owns me, but Big D has my back and watches out for me. He makes sure nobody takes advantage of me."

"Who's watching him?"

I don't reply. I gaze at the floor with tears threatening to form in my eyes. This is not how I anticipated our reunion would be.

He seems to note my sadness, and clears his throat. "How have you and your mother been? Is she still with that Puerto Rican guy?"

"She's not with Carlos right now, but we've been okay."

"I'm glad."

"How . . . how have you been?" Is this an appropriate question to ask of someone who just got out of jail? I have no idea.

"I'm good. Been working hard. Got some business deals going that are really going to pay off."

"That's good."

"Yeah, I saw you on TV when I was locked up. That show on BET. The video show."

"*106 & Park*?"

"Yeah, that's the one. I saw you and Dreya, and I knew

you were finally gonna do it. All that singing you did as a little girl was gonna pay off."

I'm still tripping off the fact that my daddy was watching me on TV in jail. This is a wow moment.

"Yeah, that was a really big deal for us."

"And I never knew Dreya had all that attitude! She was working the crowd."

My dad jumps up off the couch and does a pretty good imitation of Dreya's dancing. I cover my mouth, but the laugh still escapes.

He says, "I wish I had known you were so talented. You could've retired your mama a long time ago from that post office."

"Better late than never, huh?"

He sits back down. "Yeah, I hope so. . . ."

Crap. Crap, crap, crap. I didn't mean to say that. Especially since he's a latecomer to the Sunday Tolliver show. It just kinda leaked out.

"You know, I always managed to make sure you and Shawn were okay," my dad says. "You might not know about it, but I did send money when I could."

"I honestly don't know. My mom has never said anything about it one way or the other."

My Aunt Charlie on the other hand . . . well, let's just say . . . every negative thing I've ever heard about my father came out of her mouth. She can't stand him and she doesn't have a problem telling the world.

"Well, Shawn always was a sweetheart. I should've known she wouldn't talk bad about me."

"Can I ask you a question?" I ask.

"Anything. Ask me anything."

"Why are you coming around now? It's not that I'm not happy to see you, but why now?"

"Because I don't want to see these big-time record executives pimp you. And they will if you let them. Plus, I heard some bull popped off in New York. If Carlos and his crew put you in danger again, there will be hell to pay."

"So you're not just interested in the money?" I hate that I have to ask this question, but I feel like if I don't, I'll be kicking myself later for not asking it.

"Nah, I don't need your money. I'm set right now. As a matter of fact . . . naw, never mind."

"What? Tell me."

He links his fingers together and cracks his knuckles. "Well, I wasn't gonna say anything about this, because if I know your mother, she'll try to give the money back."

"What money?"

"I sent you that twenty-five-thousand-dollar check."

Now it's my turn to jump out of my seat. "What? *You* sent the money?"

"Yeah, Bryce told me what happened with Carlos, and I couldn't let your college fund go up in smoke like that."

I shake my head. This isn't making any sense. Why would Bryce tell my father anything about this, and why would Bryce care to try to help Carlos in his money issues?

"Bryce told you what? That he stole my college fund from Carlos?"

My father chuckles and pats the seat next to him. "Is that what you think happened?"

I nod. "Carlos told my mom that Bryce was going to let him buy a stake in the club for twenty-five thousand dollars, and that when it was time for the deal to go down Bryce reneged, and shot Carlos."

"He's leaving out some very crucial elements from the story."

I sit back down. "Like what?"

"Like the fact that it was fifty thousand for him to buy a stake in the club. He was trying to gamble your college fund to get the rest of the money."

"I don't believe this."

My father ignores my protest and keeps talking. "When he lost nearly all of your money, he and his cousins tried to strong-arm Bryce. They came in his club with guns blazing, thinking they were going to force Bryce to sign over a portion of the club's profits to Carlos."

No, no, no! This cannot be true! If it's true, then it means that the man my mother loves stole my money plain and simple. That's probably the real reason why he refuses to show his face. He's probably guilty as all get-out.

"My mom would be very upset if she heard about this."

"That's why you shouldn't tell her. I probably shouldn't have told you. I just don't want you thinking that Bryce and LaKeisha are the enemy. Bryce told me y'all have beef, but you and his little brother just got caught in the cross fire of all this."

"What did you have to do with it?" I ask. It seems like he has too many details to have just heard about this. I could be one-hundred-percent wrong, but it just doesn't seem to make sense.

"I didn't have anything to do with that. Bryce and I go way back. Plus we have a mutual dislike for Carlos. Carlos did his sister dirty, and was messing with my ex-wife."

"So you're telling me that this whole time I've believed Bryce was the villain and it was really Carlos? Bryce is the good guy?"

My father laughs. "I don't know if I'd call him the good guy. He's just not the one who made your college fund disappear."

"Well . . . I know you just want to help and all, but really my mom has got my back on the music thing. I don't know if it would be a good idea for you to get in the mix. Let me get through this reality show and maybe we can talk about it again."

I don't know why I can't just come out and say no. Maybe I'm ashamed that I don't trust my own father enough to be a part of my career. But that's the truth. I don't trust him, because I don't really know him.

Is that bad?

"I guess that's your choice," he says. "But just know that I'm there if you need me. Give me your cell phone so I can put my number in there."

It's crazy that my father's number is not already in my cell phone. Or that my mother wouldn't have known how to contact him if we had an emergency. And why isn't he asking for my number too? Why should I have to do all of the calling? He's the father. He should call me, right?

"I'm so proud of you, Sunday."

"Because I have a record deal?"

"Yes, but not just that. I'm proud that you are going to college and that you turned out so well. I brag about you all the time."

Well, this is something. I've never heard this from my dad before. Now that I think about it, I've never heard it from a man before.

"Thanks, Dad."

"Well, your mom told me you were on your way out of the country in a couple days."

"You called my mom?"

He laughs out loud. "No, Shawn called me. Threatened my life! She told me that I better not stand you up over here."

I can't help but smile. My mom always holds it down for me. "You know how my mom is. She's a ride-or-die chick."

"Yeah, I miss Shawn. Hate that things didn't work out between us! But we did one thing right."

"Really?" I ask. "What's that?"

"We made you, baby girl."

My father stands to his feet. "Well, I don't want to take up too much of your time. I know you've got work to do."

I feel a lump in my throat the size of a golf ball. I don't want him to go. It's been less than an hour and I haven't seen him in years.

"Do you . . . um . . . want to get something to eat, Daddy? Shelly made us some grub, but if you don't want to stay here we can go somewhere else. My treat."

My dad pulls me from the couch and into a hug. "I would love to go out to eat with my favorite girl. And there is no way I'd make you treat! You like Chinese?"

I nod.

"Then let's see if we can find some General Tso's chicken around here!"

I'm still feeling really good about spending the afternoon and evening with my dad. But I knew I was going to have to come home and give my mom a rundown of what took place. So I did. Well, I gave an edited version.

And even though it wasn't the entire story, my mom and Aunt Charlie sit on our living room couch, staring at me in shock. I just told them that my dad is the one who sent me the twenty-five-thousand check for my tuition. My mother looks especially twisted, so I decide not to mention anything about what my dad said about Carlos. He's not in the picture now anyway, so it doesn't really matter.

My mom says, "So, I guess he thinks that's gonna make up for all the lost time, huh? He can have his check. I don't want his money. He can have it back."

"Girl, have you lost your mind?" Aunt Charlie asks. "Sending some money this way is the least he could do."

"No. The least he could've done was . . ." My mother closes her eyes and sighs. I can tell she wants to go into a rant on my dad, but she never does.

"Mom, I'm old enough to realize he hasn't been around. Nothing you say or don't say will change that fact. I already know."

"It's just frustrating," my mother says with a sigh, "when he could be doing so much more."

"At least he got caught up on his back child support," Aunt Charlie says.

"That's if he even gave Sunday that money. I'm still thinking that Carlos found a way to get us that money. I don't have any proof that it's from Jonah."

"Mom, how can you even talk about giving the money back when you said it was a blessing? Can't you just view it that way? My dad trying to bless me for a change."

My mom's eyebrows furrow into a little frown. "I see Jonah made a great impression on you. He's a charmer, isn't he? You look just like him too."

I don't answer my mom's question. It sounds rhetorical. Plus it seems like a setup. Like how could I give the right answer? I feel like she'll be irritated with my answer either way. Plus, I don't want my mother to know that I believe my dad. I also don't want her to know how glad I was to see him.

"Well, what he won't be doing is managing my career," I say, hoping this will get rid of the tension in the room.

"You dang skippy," Aunt Charlie says. "I don't know why he even thought he was gonna get that off."

I shrug. "Me either. He warned me about Big D. I guess he doesn't really care for him, but it is what it is. Big D hasn't done me wrong yet."

"Darius is a good guy," my mother says. "He's got your back."

I lift an eyebrow in my mother's direction. If what my

father says about Carlos is true, I really can't trust her instinct on who is a good guy and who isn't. For some reason, what my father says rings true, too. I think it's because I can't think of a good reason for him to lie, and when I think back on how Carlos showed up in Philly looking like the walking dead . . . well, I just didn't have a good feeling about that.

"I shouldn't even be talking to you, Sunday," Aunt Charlie says.

"What did I do?"

"You didn't convince your record company to send me to Barbados with y'all."

I roll my eyes and sit on my mother's recliner. "Aunt Charlie, it wasn't Epsilon Records. It was BET. They are filming the reality show down there and they want it to be really positive."

"You trying to say I'm not positive?"

"I'm not saying anything. BET thinks that you are too much for the tween and teen audience. I didn't have anything to do with it."

"But you could've put your foot down, Sunday."

"Are you kidding me? I had to beg them to let Dreya come. They didn't want her on the show either, because of Truth's drama."

Aunt Charlie's eyes widen as she looks at my mom. "You hear this, Shawn? Sunday is running things now."

"Charlie, you don't need to go anyway. Let these kids have their fun. It's the summer of their senior year, Sunday's about to go off to college soon. Stop trying to relive your teen years through these kids."

"You are dead wrong for that, Shawn. Dead wrong. You've got a career and a retirement plan. What do I have?"

"Charlie, I know you are not trying to make a career out of this reality-show thing."

"Why not? If they let Flavor Flav have a reality show, I could dang sure have one. I'm much more entertaining than he is."

Now this conversation has entered the land of certifiably crazy. This is why I'm glad Aunt Charlie is not coming to Barbados. I'm looking forward to this trip, even though I'm going to be working really hard on the video shoot.

"They do have you staying at an all-inclusive, right?" my mother asks.

"Yep. We're staying at the Almond Resort. It's right on Casuarina Beach."

Aunt Charlie sucks her teeth. "As if we know where that is, smarty pants."

My mom elbows Aunt Charlie in the side. "Stop tripping. There will be other vacations."

"I think we should go to the Caribbean for Christmas, Mom. What do you think?"

"I would love that, baby."

I'm glad that my mom is smiling again and not thinking about my dad anymore. Aunt Charlie is another story, though.

She says, "You just make sure that your cousin is represented on this show. She's feeling really low about not being with Truth right now. Y'all need to pull together and help her feel better."

"The only one who can make Dreya feel better is herself, Aunt Charlie. She's got to stop thinking about Truth."

My mom says, "You got that right. Once she stops thinking about Truth, she can get over him, and once she gets over him . . ."

"She can move on to the next one," Aunt Charlie says.

My mother shakes her head and sighs. "I was going to say that once she gets over him, she can make a plan for her own success."

Aunt Charlie rolls her eyes. "Oh, yeah. You and your daughter are just so positive! It's enough positivity in the room between the two of you to give us world peace or something."

"That sounds like a hater comment," I say.

My mother nods in agreement. "I think your aunt needs a group hug."

"You heffas better not hug me."

My mom winks and I rush over to the couch and plop down next to Aunt Charlie. We squeeze her tight from both angles, giving her plenty of the Tolliver love.

Aunt Charlie says, "I'm still mad!"

But I don't believe her, because she's laughing out loud!

12

We leave for Barbados tomorrow. Score! I am excited beyond words. I've never been on an island. Shoot, I've never been out of the country. This music-industry thing has some real perks.

But before we go, I think it's important for me to have a heart-to-heart talk with Sam. I want us to have a real drama-free good time in the islands. He's the only real friend I've got going on this trip, and I want us to have a good time.

He's taking me to an interview at the radio station this morning. Hot 107.9 is interviewing me, Dreya, and Truth about our reality show, which premieres tonight. Sam is tagging along because I asked him to go to the aquarium with me this afternoon.

Sam's driving today, because I don't feel like driving. His raggedy SUV could use some pimping, but I'm not enough of a diva to even care. He pulls onto I-20 headed toward downtown Atlanta, and I sit back and get ready to enjoy the early-morning traffic. We have to be on air for the morning drive-time show, which Big D says is a big spot.

"How is Dreya getting to the radio station?" Sam asks. "I could've picked her up."

I laugh out loud. I may not be too much of a diva to roll around in the rustmobile, but Dreya most certainly is.

"She probably drove herself, if Big D didn't come and get her."

Sam replies, "Or Truth might've scooped her."

"They're not supposed to be seeing one another, so I don't think that's the case."

Sam raises his eyebrows and focuses on the road. "Alrighty then."

"What are you saying?"

"I'm not saying anything."

I poke Sam in the ribs. "You better not be keeping anything from me, Sam. I'm not playing with you."

"Okay, okay! Let's just say that they may not be following the rules one hundred percent."

I plop back in my seat and let out a huge sigh. I knew that Dreya was being too cool about this breakup thing. When she's around Aunt Charlie and my mom, she acts all sad, but when we're at the studio or anywhere else, she's just fine.

"She's still seeing him, isn't she?"

Sam nods. "Yep. He spent the night at her crib last night."

Dreya is so stupid. She is going to let her toxic relationship with Truth mess up everything we've worked so hard to achieve. And he's not even worth it! Dreya saw the reality show! She saw Truth caught in the act with Bethany.

Somebody needs to explain this to me like I'm a two-year-old because I just don't understand.

"The aquarium thing this afternoon. What's that about?" Sam asks. "I know it's not a date, so I'm just trying to figure out where I stand."

"I see you changing the subject, Sam."

He gives me a warm smile. "It's just that I don't want to spend my alone time with you talking about Truth and Dreya's played-out selves."

"Alone time? Wow, Sam . . ."

"Are we not alone?"

"You are thirsty."

"Parched."

I swallow hard. It's very difficult for me to be in close confines with Sam when he starts cranking up the crush machine. It just went from zero crush to three-sixty crush up in this automobile. Where is the escape hatch when I need it?

After taking a moment to compose myself, I reply, "You're right, Sam. The aquarium thing is not a date. Actually, it's a play date."

"A play date?"

"Yes. Like when two moms set up an afternoon of activities for their kiddies."

Sam laughs out loud. "What if I'm not playing?"

I grin at him and refuse to play into his flirtation. "Well, can it just be about us hanging out before the next round of reality-show madness?"

"Yep. It sure can."

"Good."

A light rain starts to fall, so Sam turns on his windshield wipers. "You know Bethany recorded one of our songs, right? Did I tell you that?"

"Really? How did it turn out?" I ask.

"Hot. She really did her thing. I can't even lie."

"I knew she'd do well. Do you think Epsilon will give her a record deal too?"

Sam shrugs as he leans forward to peer through the window. The rain is coming down just a little bit harder. "Maybe not Epsilon. She's not really their kind of artist."

"Well, we should really try to push that. She could get us paid too."

Sam chuckles. "Now who's thirsty?"

"Yeah, parched!" I reply. "Are you ready for Barbados?"

"Am I ready for you to be Dilly's love interest? Um . . ."

"Sam . . . it's just for the video."

Sam nods. "I know. And he's in love with Bethany. How do you think she's gonna feel about that?"

I shouldn't care about how Bethany feels about anything. "She should be glad that her boyfriend is still in the mix after everything that's happened."

"So you and Dilly made up? I don't have to worry about breaking my foot off in his behind?"

"We're straight. Actually . . ."

I start to tell Sam about the meeting with my dad and

what he said about Carlos being the villain—just like Dilly had been saying all along. But for some reason, I change my mind. Maybe it's because I don't know if I really believe that or maybe I'm just not ready to bring Sam all up in that mix yet.

"This is our exit," Sam says. "I'm surprised we didn't get caught in a lot of traffic."

"Yeah, me too."

Sam pulls off of the freeway and drives toward Turner Field. This is my first in-studio radio interview. All of the others I've had have been on the telephone. Mystique offered to come with us, but Dreya and I decided that we didn't need her there.

When we get to the radio-station parking lot, I see Truth's Impala, but I don't see Dreya's car. This is not a good sign. It means that what Sam said is true. They are back together.

Aunt Charlie's gonna flip out.

We step into the building and see Truth and Dreya sitting together in a chair that only has room for one. Dreya looks up at me and gives me a wicked smile.

"Don't say anything, Sunday," Dreya says.

"What would I say?"

"I don't know, but whatever it is you're thinking, please keep it to yourself."

The receptionist shows us up to the studio area where a bubbly production assistant is waiting.

"Good morning, y'all!" she says.

"Where're the DJs?" Truth asks.

"Well, as you know we've got the *Rickey Smiley Morn-*

ing Show on. They tape in Dallas, so they're going to call in here."

Sam takes a seat in the corner. He's not a part of the interview, and I don't think he has a problem with it. He takes off his hat, drops it in his lap, and leans back with his eyes closed.

I hope I don't need him to have my back during this interview!

The production assistant is pointing to where we should sit. Dreya and Truth take seats next to each other, and I sit across from them. There's a microphone in front of each of our faces.

"Okay, when I give you guys the signal, that means we're live and your microphones are hot. So don't talk bad about anybody unless you don't want the entire country to hear."

She doesn't have to worry about Truth and Dreya saying anything into the microphone. They're too busy drooling over one another. It's completely sickening. I'm tempted to text Aunt Charlie and tell her what's going on in here. But then, who needs Dreya to catch a beat-down right before we go to Barbados?

We hear the intro to the *Rickey Smiley Morning Show* over the speakers, and the production assistant gives us a thumbs-up. This must be the signal! She never said what it was going to be.

Rickey said, "We've got Sunday Tolliver, Truth, and Drama up in the spot this morning! They got a show coming on BET, and they blowing up the airwaves with number-one hits. Good morning, y'all!"

"Hey, Rickey!" Dreya says as if they go way back.

I say, "Good morning!"

Truth says, "What up, Rickey?"

"Already!" Rickey replies. "Tell us about this show! How did it get started? Is there gonna be a lot of drama? Like the Atlanta Housewives?"

Dreya says, "Rickey, you know my name, babe. Drama is as drama does."

I roll my eyes and say, "There's a little drama, but we keep it positive."

"I keep it one hundred all day every day," Truth says. "What you see from me is the realest of real."

Rickey's co-host Ebony says, "But what's this I hear about a love triangle? We all saw the YouTube video. I mean what's really going on?"

"That was *all* media hype," Dreya says. "I mean really, he's got the best of the best, so why would he need anything more? Not hatin' on my cousin, but you know."

"Yeah, that video was taken horribly out of context. There's no triangle here," I say.

Okay, for real, there was no reason for Dreya to try to dump on me. Especially when I know her man *did* want me, even if he's not trying to holla now. And how's Dreya gonna explain all this reckless talk when the BET viewers see the footage of Truth and Bethany?

"So tell us, what will we see on the show?" Rickey asks.

"A lot of fly concert footage, behind-the-scenes stuff on the tour buses . . ." I reply.

"Don't tell me there's no drama!" Ebony says. "There's got to be. It's a reality show, there's got to be some good stuff."

"Well, it's mostly under wraps, but I will tell y'all the show is crunk," Truth says.

I say, "Yeah, we're really not able to tell too much about the episodes, but it's gonna be really good."

"So, what's up next for y'all?" Rickey asks.

"Well, I'm about to shoot the video for my single 'Can U See Me' in Barbados, and we're gonna get all the behind-the-scenes footage for that too. It'll be a special on BET too."

"Can't wait to get to Barbados! Home of Rihanna!" Dreya says. "I love her. She's the only chick in the game that can hold a candle to me."

Ebony laughs out loud. "What about Mystique? She's killing the game right now."

"That's like comparing apples and oranges. She's a good singer, but I'm an all-around performer," Dreya replies.

I am so glad that this is not a television interview, because I wouldn't want them to capture the evil side-eye glare that I'm giving Dreya right now. She's tripping for real. I knew that she was mad about me getting my own show and the celebrity treatment, but she's on some old career-suicide stuff right now.

Rickey says, "Well, I want to wish y'all the best of luck with everything you're doing. I love to see positive young people on the come up."

"Thank you for having us on!" I say.

"Already!" Rickey replies.

The associate producer gives us another signal. This time she waves her hand in the air in a little flip. What the heck does that mean?

"Okay, you guys are done," the associate producer says when we don't move. "Thanks for getting up this early to hang out with us."

As soon as all four of us are back in the receptionist area, I step to Dreya. "That's the last time you gonna try to play me on radio, TV, wherever. I'm sick of your mouth."

Sam steps between us. "Come on now, not here. Let's do this somewhere else."

"We can do it right here," Dreya says. "I'm still the top chick, and you need to recognize. I think you smellin' yourself 'cause BET and Epsilon is on you extra hard right now. But I'm still number one."

"You know what, Dreya, I'm gonna leave here, before I say or do something that you might regret."

I storm out of the building and huff and puff my way to Sam's truck. He hurries to open the door for me, probably to keep me from jumping on Dreya when she and Truth come out of the building. Because I really feel like I could jump on her right now.

Sam climbs in on his side and says, "You already know that Dreya is a trip. Ain't nothing changed."

"I know, but every time we start to be okay, she does something crazy. I feel like I'm going to have to cut her off at some point."

"Nah, that's your family. You won't cut her off. But you don't have to keep doing nice stuff for her."

He's so right about that. I remember feeling bad that BET only wanted the next show to feature me, and how I pushed really hard to have her on. And now she just throws it right back in my face like she doesn't appreciate anything.

Before Sam pulls off, Dreya runs up to my window and says, "I know what you did, Sunday. Truth told me all about him and Bethany, and how you *knew* they were getting it on."

So this is why she's tripping. I roll the window down.

"Yeah, I knew. And I asked Bethany to stop! Your boyfriend was hooking up with her in exchange for tracks! How can you be okay with him and be mad at me?"

"Because you are my cousin! You should've told me about it. Why should I find out on TV that my roommate is messing with my man?"

"I was trying to protect you, Dreya! If I had known it was gonna be on the show, I would've told you."

"You still foul though, because you're writing songs for Bethany. How could you help her after what she's done to me?"

"That's business. It's not personal."

"It's all personal, Sunday. When are you gonna figure that out?"

Dreya walks away from the truck looking dejected and leaving me feeling like a rat. Every time I do something to protect the people that I love it ends up going all wrong. Maybe the same thing happened to Mystique and that's the reason she's only got her mother and her man to rely on.

That is not going to happen to me.

"You want to go to Busy Bee's Café for some breakfast, Sunday?" Sam asks.

"I look like I need food?"

He chuckles. "You look like you need something."

I need something, all right. Can I get an order of cool-best-friend-like cousin and a side of almost boyfriend? Then I'd like to top it off with a chocolate-covered Mommy-I-can't-stand-Dreya-right-now. . . .

13

"So, I asked you to come here with me today because I want to tell you something," I say to Sam.

Sam and I are sitting in my favorite place in the aquarium. In front of the whale exhibit. My whales are so peaceful, and I think they know when I'm here. Well, I'd like to think that they do, but most probably they don't know I'm alive.

I think it freaks Sam out to come here with me, because this is where we had our first kiss. It's a good memory for me, but not Sam, because he's been trying to get me to claim him as my boyfriend ever since.

"How'd it go when you met up with your dad?" Sam asks.

"Better than I expected, that's for sure."

"You had Big D scared for a minute. He was tripping when you left with your dad. He thought you were going to let him manage you after that."

"Are you for real? He didn't say anything about that to me."

"He told me he was real twisted."

I give Sam an emphatic head shake. "Nah. He's got nothing to worry about. I might be looking for a daddy, but I'm not looking for a new manager."

"That's a good thing for Big D."

"Sam, aren't you going to ask what I came here to tell you?"

"What do you want to tell me, Sunday?" Sam asks.

I totally wish I could click the dislike button on Sam's attitude-filled tone of voice. He has absolutely no faith in me at all, I see. He's just assuming the worst from jump. I'm not liking this.

"First, thank you for breakfast. Gotta love Busy Bee's Café."

Sam chuckles. "Yeah, and you're greedy too. If Epsilon wasn't paying for this whole Barbados adventure on account of you, I woulda made you split the bill with me."

"Yeah, right. You invited me out," I say. "How you gonna try to make me pay?"

"I guess you're right. Next time you can pay for me."

I laugh. "I don't take guys out on dates."

"Well, that's perfect, because we don't go on dates, right? We go on play dates."

"Yes, that's true, only play dates. We'll have real ones soon."

Sam gives a big belly laugh. "Don't go there today, Sunday. What did you want to ask me?"

"I just want to know if you're going to be cool with Dilly being my male lead in the video."

He shrugs. It is a noncommittal shrug. The kind that tells me absolutely nothing about what he's thinking, which is all bad, because if he didn't care, he'd give me a more concrete clue. Big sigh . . .

"Why wouldn't I be cool? He's your label mate. That's how Epsilon rolls. They're trying to parlay this into a career move for him."

"I just want you to know that it doesn't mean anything, and you're still the one I'm digging no matter what they put on the show."

"The BET cameras can only catch things you actually do. Like there's no way Truth and Bethany can try to say that something was taken out of context when they were hemmed up backstage."

"That's true, but on the video shoot, I have to pretend that I like Dilly. I just want you to know the real."

"That's real nice of you to do that, Sunday. I feel so special."

Why the sarcasm? Why the side-eye glances? Does Sam not want this? When did Sam stop wanting to be my boyfriend? It must've been like thirty seconds ago, because I swear on the way down here he was trying to turn my invitation into a date.

"Sam, why are you tripping?" I ask.

"Because you keep playing games and I'm just super tired. You act like I'm supposed to get excited because you say you're digging me, when I know you do, but not more than your cash money."

"That's not fair, Sam. I met you chasing my music career. Don't act like you didn't know that about me from day one."

"I did know that about you, but I thought that at some point you'd put that cold chick to rest and be my girl-friend. But I'm the only one getting personal. The cold chick is all bidness, right?"

"I'm not all business."

"Then why haven't we gone on more than one real date since the tour? I felt like we really got close, espe-cially when Dilly almost got kidnapped. But we get back home and have one date. I'm sick of sounding like a chump over you."

"I don't want to argue, Sam. . . ."

"Then let's not argue. Let's just stop going in circles."

I swallow a huge mouthful of air. Not on purpose, but because I opened my mouth to speak and nothing came out.

Sam's entire body seems to sigh. "Look, Sunday. I want us to go to Barbados to hang out, have a good time, kick it, and groove to some dance-hall music. But don't make it seem like it means something. That carrot you keep dangling in front of my nose is rotten, and it's got mold on it."

"That's gross, Sam."

"Well, that's all I've got right now. You and Dilly are the lyrical wonder twins. I don't speak in rhymes."

Sam stands up from our bench in front of the whale tank. He's just turned the most tranquil and peaceful place in the world into a drama-filled hot mess.

"You ready to go? I've still got some packing to do," Sam says.

I nod because I don't know what other response to give. I wish I could say that I'm not ready to go, because

I really am not. I still feel the need to have the last word in this conversation.

"I'm sorry, Sam. I didn't mean to take you in circles."

He nods, but his lips are in a tight grim-looking line. "Well, I'm walking in a straight line now."

What does this even mean? Does it mean he's walking away from me? I want us to walk together, but it sounds like he's got a head start and plans on leaving me in the dust.

Everything's personal.

14

Everyone meets up at Big D's so that we can ride to the airport in limos. The BET cameras are here too, because this will begin their footage. Since I see how they like to flip stuff around, I'm going to be extra careful this time. They're not going to catch me slipping this time around.

All of our bags are piled near the door, and seriously, for us to be going on a four-day trip, there is way too much baggage. Dreya has two big suitcases, a carry-on, and a trunk. I've only got two bags, but Mystique really takes the cake. She's got three big suitcases, and two trunks.

I guess nobody had to tell Mystique to be ready for the cameras. She's got a full face of makeup on, including fake mink eyelashes. She's got a new lace-front wig too. Long, blond, and full of curls. She most definitely is picture perfect and ready for her close-up.

I don't have on a stitch of makeup, and my hair is up in a ponytail. I see our makeup artist Regina, glaring at me from across the room, because she's been trying to get me to sit down in the chair, but I won't. I don't want to be on the plane with my face spray-painted on. I hope the BET viewers like the natural look, because that's what they're getting.

I ask, "Mystique, what do you have in those trunks?"

"Shoes."

"But we're going to Barbados. . . . Isn't there going to be mostly sand everywhere?"

Mystique smiles. "Sure, but I'll probably go clubbing, and I have no idea what I'll be in the mood to wear. Zac usually takes me dancing."

"Where is Zac anyway? Is he going to fly down with us?"

"No," Mystique replies. "He's in London right now, doing a promotional tour with one of his artists. He's going to meet us there on Saturday. Then, he and I are staying for an additional week after y'all leave."

"Must be nice," I say.

She nods and grins. "Yeah. We need a vacay. It's the third anniversary of us getting together, so we're going to celebrate big. I'm going to lie down for a little bit before we leave. I'm utterly fatigued."

Mystique leaves the room with a little dramatic flourish. It seems like I'm the only one who didn't come fully prepared for the cameras.

I scan the room to try and guess what everyone's thinking. Bethany and Dilly are in one corner listening to one iPod. It's like they're joined at the wire or something.

Sam is being his normal chill self, and Dreya . . . well Dreya is reading a magazine, but she keeps looking up like she's waiting for something. Maybe she just feels some kind of way about Truth not coming with us, especially since they're back together now.

I want to say something to Sam, but it's like walking on eggshells with him right now. I wish he'd kept his thoughts to himself yesterday. Way to put a damper on our trip.

"What's wrong with you?" Dreya asks as she drops her magazine at her side.

I watch the BET cameraman zoom in like he's about to get that good-good. No sir. Not today!

"I'm cool, just trying to get my mind right for this video shoot. What was it like when you and Truth shot the video for 'What You Gonna Do'?"

"Well, we weren't on an island for our shoot. Just some abandoned warehouse. Nobody plopped down the big bucks for Truth's video."

"Okay . . . but what was it like filming the video? Did you have to do a lot of takes?"

She shakes her head. "Nope. Only a couple. The cameraman was only paid for a few hours so we pretty much had to be spot on."

Dreya is on some other stuff, I see. I don't know what she's trying to prove by calling out Epsilon Records on BET. They have done right by her. She's a new artist, so it's not like they're gonna be spending millions of dollars on her videos. Shoot, the only reason we're going to Barbados is because of the reality show. Dreya knows this too, so her hateration is so unnecessary.

Dreya's phone buzzes, and she walks outside to answer it. I plop down in one of Big D's white leather chairs next to Shelly, who's reading a book. She's picture perfect too and wearing a white catsuit with a tiny jean half vest, and six-inch heels. Who wears that to the airport?

"Hey, Shelly. What are you reading?"

"A grown-folk book. Nothing you need to be concerned with."

"Wow . . . okay. Have you been to Barbados before? Is the food good?"

Shelly laughs. "No. I've been to Jamaica and to the Bahamas. Not Barbados. What's with all the questions?"

"I'm excited, I guess! I just want to go. I've never even been on a plane before."

"Seriously?"

I nod. "I haven't been anywhere, really. So this is gonna be fun."

I'm trying to convince myself of this, even if I've got Sam looking a melancholy mess and Dreya seemingly hell-bent on causing friction.

Big D and Mystique come into the room, and Big D is holding a big trash bag.

"I thought you were lying down," I say to Mystique.

She replies, "I was, but this is much more exciting."

"Guess what this is," Big D says.

"I have no idea, Big D," I reply.

"It's fan mail. Epsilon Records forwarded this over this morning."

Dreya looks up from her magazine. "Fan mail for us?"

"This bag is all Sunday's. They're going to send the

rest this week. It'll be here when we get back from Barbados."

Mystique digs in and hands me a letter. "Read one!"

"Okay." I snatch the letter open and read.

"Hi, Sunday. My name is Zoey and I love your music so much. You don't know how much your single 'Can U See Me' has helped me in my life. I was feeling really sad because my boyfriend broke up with me on Facebook. I just logged in one day and his status said that he was single. I was totally devastated. But your song helped me to see that there's more than one boy in the world and just because my boyfriend didn't see me for who I am, somebody will. I hope you write me back! Best in all you do! Love, Zoey."

Dreya gives one single hand clap. "Oh, that is so cute and precious. You've got little teenybopper fans."

"You smell like a hater right now," Mystique says.

Dreya laughs out loud. "You smell played out."

Mystique steps to Dreya. "Yeah, I heard what you said about me on the radio yesterday. You better be glad I like Sunday or you wouldn't have a record deal right now."

Dreya looks Mystique up and down. "You must be used to scaring everyone around you. It doesn't work on me, honey. You should really fall back right now."

The look on the BET producer's face is so irritating to me right now. He looks like a cat who just lucked up on an abandoned tuna-fish sandwich.

I see that Dreya is determined to make herself the star of my reality show.

"I don't have to scare anyone," Mystique replies. "My track record speaks for itself. You can talk to me when you're at the top. Matter of fact, talk to me when you're even halfway to the top. Right now, you're nothing but a one-hit wonder."

Bethany, who has removed her earbuds to listen to this, says, "Oooo, she told you!"

"Shut up, wannabe," Dreya says.

"Wanna be who? You? Girl, please. Nobody wants to be you. I've got my own sound, and it's a lot better than that screeching you do!"

Wow, Bethany is tripping! BET said that they wanted to keep this show positive, and then they want to go and cut the monkey. Let's get ready to rumble.

"You have the sound that Sunday gave you," Dreya says with a laugh. "So, I guess that means you want to be Sunday."

Mystique interjects, "Now is good a time as any, I guess, to announce that I just signed Bethany to Mystical Sounds. Sunday and Sam wrote her some slamming music, and I'm impressed. So, Drama . . . you *do* need to fall back."

My eyes widen as I make eye contact with Sam. Neither of us knew that this was in the works with Mystique. Not that I mind, but Mystique was kind of down on Bethany before. Now all of a sudden she's signing her to a deal.

It's whatever though, as long as I'm getting paid for those songs.

Sam says, "The limo bus is here."

Everyone piles into the bus, except Mystique. Her personal driver is taking her to the airport in Zac's Maybach. I guess she's too special to ride with us chickens.

When I notice Dreya frozen in place, instead of heading to the bus, I say, "Dreya, are you okay?"

"Yeah, I'm cool. I'm just trying to figure out why everyone keeps helping that tramp Bethany. Mystique didn't even like her before, but all because you wrote her some songs, now she's a hot property."

Dreya says that she's cool, but she doesn't sound cool. She sounds mad as the place the devil calls home.

"Did you forget that Bethany has a great voice? That's why we were all singing together, Dreya. She's got that husky contralto, and she kind of sounds like Toni Braxton and Norah Jones all wrapped into one."

"She might have a good voice, but she doesn't have any stage presence. She's just an average white chick. Ain't like she's got Kim Kardashian's looks or anything. She's more like Britney Spears on a bad day."

See, this is why Dreya will never be on top. She can't focus on her own stuff because she's so busy hating on the next chick.

"Why does it matter to you if Bethany gets a record deal? She doesn't sing anything like what you sing. Y'all will have completely different fan bases."

Dreya gives me an indignant glare. An "Are you serious?" mean mug.

"Why would I want her to be successful?" Dreya asks. "She lived in my apartment and hooked up with my boyfriend."

"But he's supposed to be your ex-boyfriend anyway. So what does that matter?"

"Because you, my mom, or Auntie Shawn don't tell me

what to do. Truth is my current and gonna be my forever, boyfriend."

"Okay, okay. But can we please get in the limo bus before we miss our flight?"

"Yeah, but know this. I will do whatever I can to make Bethany fail. That is a promise."

No doubt, I believe her, but Dreya better be careful. Now that Mystique's signed Bethany to a record deal, Bethany belongs to Mystique. And trying to bring Bethany down will mean putting a dent in Mystique's wallet.

Somehow . . . I don't think Dreya will come out on top in a battle with Mystique. And what's more, I don't want to be stuck in the middle of it all.

15

Oh heck no. I do not *even* believe this mess. But I cannot flip out the way I want to, because our BET camera crew is steady filming and waiting for a reaction.

We're at our gate about to board our flight to Barbados, and guess who runs up to us and into Dreya's arms?

If you guessed Truth . . . you win. Although, I don't know what you win. I can't even think of a prize right now, because I'm so mad.

"Epsilon Records is *not* paying for him to be on this trip," Mystique complains. "He is an Epsilon artist, but he is not on the budget for this."

"Simmer down, Ma," Truth says. "I'm paying my own way. Ain't no way I'm sending my baby to Barbados where some island men can behold her beauty and try to hook up with her."

"I ain't goin' nowhere, Daddy," Dreya says.

Daddy! OMG! I am so mad right now, I could choke.

Not only is Aunt Charlie going to break her foot off in my butt (even though I had nothing to do with Truth coming), but now BET is going to be mad that this nearly convicted felon is a part of the show they wanted to keep positive.

Big D says, "Man . . . I thought we talked about this."

"We did talk about it. You told me Epsilon wasn't paying for me and I said cool. End of conversation. Why you act like I don't have my own money?"

"Where are you staying on the island?" Sam asks.

"I got a suite for me and my boo at the Almond Resort, where y'all are staying. She told me Sunday was putting my queen up in a tiny room."

Okay, now I'm beyond mad. I'm furious. Why do they keep blaming me for stuff that is totally out of my control?

"I didn't pick the rooms, the travel coordinator at Epsilon Records did," I reply.

Truth says, "Same thing, but it's all good because I rectified that situation."

"Yeah, my Aunt Charlie is gonna rectify your situation when she finds out about this."

Truth laughs out loud. "Your auntie doesn't scare me. I took an anger-management class last weekend. I'm all cured."

"You took one class and you're cured?" I ask.

"Sunday, stop," Dreya says. "He's cool, okay. Stop bringing up the past. I've forgiven him for everything, so why can't everyone else just move on?"

"Yeah, Sunday, I'm cool," Truth says. Then he cocks his head to one side and asks, "Did you forget to comb your hair today, Sunday? Didn't you know you were gonna be on TV?"

One hand goes self-consciously to my ponytail, as I mumble, "Shut up, Truth."

Then Truth pulls Dreya directly in front of the camera so that he can kiss her. I so want to puke right now.

Dilly, who's been eerily quiet up until now, pulls me by the shirtsleeve down the airport concourse and toward the Dunkin' Donuts, which I had been expertly avoiding up until now. There's no way I'm going to get on that plane without a glazed donut now.

"Sunday, I don't feel comfortable with him here, and you're the only one that can make him disappear," Dilly says.

"How can I make him disappear?" I ask. "If Big D can't make him go away, I know you don't think he's gonna listen to me."

Dilly narrows his eyes. "Look at her. This is what I'm talking about."

I guess Bethany thinks no one is paying any attention to her staring Truth down. After an extra-long moment, she looks away with a hurt and pouty expression on her face.

"Maybe she's just mad because he's here," I say.

"Or maybe she's still digging him. I've been thinking that the only reason she stopped messing with him is because you caught her."

"There may be some logic to that, Dilly, but I think she really likes you now."

He folds his arms and leans on the wall. "I don't know,

Sunday. What if she only got with me because she didn't have anybody else? Maybe she's just an industry chick."

I bite my lip and chew on this theory for a minute. It is true that Bethany has, in the past, been a one-hundred-percent groupie chick. But that logic doesn't hold any water in this situation because Dilly hasn't even come up yet. He's still on the come up.

"But Dilly, she's got a record deal now. If she didn't really like you, she wouldn't be with you. She doesn't need you to make it in the industry. She's already on."

Dilly looks relieved, as if he hadn't thought of this small fact. "Thanks, Sunday. I needed that pep talk."

"No problem, dude. Anytime."

"So what about you and Sam? He's not looking like a happy camper right now. Did y'all have a fight?"

I guess since I offered Dilly relationship advice, he thinks it's okay to get all up in my Kool-Aid and he doesn't even know the flavor (yeah, I know that's old school, but it fit). Sam *does* look twisted: slouched down in an airport chair, iPod on with earbuds in, and rocking back and forth to a beat that no one else can hear.

"Sam and I are fine. He's just getting his game face on," I explain.

But Sam and I are not fine, and I keep trying to think of a way to get us there. I dismiss Dilly and order two glazed doughnuts from Dunkin' Donuts.

Once I have the tasty treats in my hand, I bustle past the canoodling Trauma (my nickname for Truth + Drama) and plop down next to Sam. He keeps bobbing his head, but turns to look at me. Without cracking a smile or anything, he looks forward again, never missing a beat.

I tap him on the arm. "Sam!"

Slowly, he removes his earbuds. He takes a deep breath, exhales it, and then finally turns to me again. "Yeah, Sunday?"

"I thought you might want one." I hand him the Dunkin' Donuts bag.

He looks down at it as if it's some kind of poison and then hands it back to me. "I'm cool. Thanks anyway."

"Well, I'll just stay here and keep you company then, if you don't mind."

Sam chuckles. "Don't you have some gold coins to count, Scrooge McSunday?"

"Cute. And no, I just want to sit here and sweat you."

Now Sam's chuckle turns into a full-fledged laugh. "Stop playing, Sunday. You don't sweat anybody, unless they smell like new dollar bills."

"That is my favorite cologne, Sam. I'm glad you recognize. But, I also enjoy the Burberry you're rocking right now."

"Is this reality TV?" Sam asks. "Because it feels so scripted. You're trying too hard, Sunday."

I nod and swallow back the sarcastic answer that I want to give. Because one, I kinda deserve it, and two, I'm not ready for Sam to walk the straight line up outta my life.

"Sam, do you think I didn't hear what you said yesterday?" I ask.

"I don't know. . . ."

"Well, I did. I get it. The carrot is old and moldy, and the circles are played out. Got it."

Sam lifts one eyebrow. "So, what is this?"

"This is me trying to holla at you."

"Is it for the cameras or is it for real?" Sam whispers.

I whisper back. "I don't do anything for the cameras. Forget them cameras. I'm only thinking about you right now."

Sam's caramel-colored cheeks redden. "I want to believe you, but . . ."

"But what?"

"But, I've gotten my hopes up before, and I've been the one looking foolish."

A tired sigh comes from my body. "I know, Sam. Can you just trust me this time?"

Sam shakes his head. "I wish I could, Sunday, but I can't."

I sit back in the chair and take a bite of the doughnut that Sam wouldn't accept. He puts his earbuds back in, leans forward with his elbows on his knees, and starts bobbing his head again.

Have I really given Sam the run-around so many times that he can't trust me at all?

I think back on the first time Sam and I were in the studio and how we vibed from the very beginning. But maybe that's not enough. Maybe we met too soon—like maybe ten years from now would've been better.

Because it seems like now, there have been too many feelings hurt. Too many egos have been bruised.

A voice comes over the loudspeaker. "Now boarding American Airlines flight nine seven one to Miami, Florida. We are now boarding first-class passengers, and passengers with small children."

I stand to my feet and grab my carry-on bag. I'm flying

first class with Mystique, Big D, and Shelly, but everyone else, including Dreya, is flying coach.

"Where are you going?" Dreya asks. "You traveling with a small child or something?"

"Ha ha ha, Dreya. You know what it is. Don't front."

Her face turns dark. "This is some mess."

"Don't worry about it, babe," Truth says. "You know what we've got to do."

She nods. "You're right, baby. I'm sticking to the plan."

Plan? Oh boy, this should be good. I just can't wait to see what they come up with!

If that sounded sarcastic, it was entirely on purpose.

16

A nudge in the ribs from Mystique awakens me from a very deep and satisfying sleep. Well, as deep and satisfying as one can get on an airplane. I don't think my first flight should've been first class. Because these big leather seats have ruined me for those sardine seats in coach. Note to self: Always request first-class flights.

"Why are you waking me up?" A string of drool goes from my hand to the side of my face.

"Eww . . ." Mystique says. "Look out the window."

I glance out the window and gasp at the sight of almost endless clear blue water. "It's beautiful," I say.

"You see that little speck of green?" Mystique asks.

"Yeah, what's that?"

"That's Barbados."

My eyes widen. "That little speck of green is the entire island?"

"Yes. It'll look bigger as we come in for landing."

I laugh out loud. "I hope so, because right now, it doesn't even look like this plane will fit on the island."

It does indeed fit, and less than an hour later, we're flying close to the island, and I can see blue water lapping against white sand. It's the most beautiful and breathtaking thing I've ever seen in my life.

Finally, we touch down at the Grantley Adams International Airport. From the outside I can tell that it's small. Like a hundred of this airport could fit in Hartsfield-Jackson International back home in the A.

As we go through customs, I notice lots of dark smiling faces. I've never seen this many black people working in one place. Some of them running the show, and others are clearly the worker bees.

I whisper to Mystique as I'm cleared in customs, "Why do they keep smiling at me?"

"You are a celebrity! A lot of these pretty black boys want to meet a pretty American girl. Sam better keep close tabs on you."

I roll my eyes. "Yeah right. Sam isn't checking for me right now. He said I had him going in circles."

"You did. But that's what girls do. Sam's going to have to realize that. Girls who are worth having are worth going in circles for."

Something about Mystique's logic is flawed, but I can't put my finger on what it is. Oh, wait, yes, I can! She sounds *crazy*!

I try to ignore the pretty Bajan girl grinning in Sam's face. She's supermodel tall, with skin the color of charcoal briquettes. Her hair is in an intricate cornrow pattern to the back, and it looks like she bought her airport uniform two sizes too little.

She says something that must be uproariously funny to Sam, because he throws his head back and laughs. I want to know what she said. I want to storm over and ask him right now. I take one step in their direction, and Mystique grabs my arm.

"Don't do it. He's flirting with that girl on purpose. He's trying to make you jealous."

"It's working," I reply.

Mystique shakes her head. "No, Sunday. You can't let him know that it's getting to you. Stay aloof and disconnected if you want him back."

This I don't understand. How does staying aloof and disconnected work to get anyone back? That seems like it would have the opposite effect. But what do I know? I'm just stupid me who drove away the best crush ever.

It takes Big D and Truth an additional amount of time to get through customs. I guess the airport crew must've heard about Truth's arrest.

After everyone is done, we head for the two stretch limos waiting for us in the ground transportation area.

"Aren't these nice?" Mystique asks me as everyone makes a mad dash for one or the other.

"They are! Did you have something to do with this?"

"Zac paid for them. He said that he wanted me and the Epsilon artists to show up to our resort in style."

"That's what's up."

I decide to go in the same limo that Sam chose, and

Mystique goes with me. I wonder if this counts as staying aloof and disconnected. I don't ask Mystique, because I'm sure that I won't want to hear her answer.

Big D, Shelly, Dilly, and Bethany are all in here too, so I guess Truth and Dreya rode with the BET crew and Regina, the makeup artist. A little grin erupts on my face when I imagine Dreya being angry about riding with "the help." Whatever, though. She should just be glad she's in Barbados!

The limos take off from the beautiful yet small airport and head toward our tropical island paradise. We were told that the resort is fifteen minutes away from the airport. And that's all we were told.

No one told me to expect the hustle and bustle of the cramped streets. Our limos seemed gargantuan trying to maneuver through the busy marketplace. On both sides of the street are people selling . . . everything! There are little wooden statues and bowls, paintings, clothes, fruit, flowers, and so much more.

"Can we get out?" I ask no one in particular.

"You'll have plenty of time to shop later," Mystique says. "We've got a video to shoot, remember?"

"Right. It's so beautiful here that I keep forgetting we're here to work."

"We'll have time to play too," Big D says.

The limo driver says, "Make sure you get to De Gap. De Reggae Lounge is good, good, good!"

"De Gap?" I ask.

"Yah, girl. St. Lawrence Gap. De Gap."

I nod with some understanding. I've read up on this little island, because who knows when I'm going to be back. St. Lawrence Gap is where all the nightlife happens.

"Zac took me to the Reggae Lounge the last time we were here. It was a hot spot!"

"Shut yuh mout. You go day?" The driver asks.

Mystique giggles and responds, "I stan day all night long. The nusic was good good."

"What did y'all just say?" Sam asks, suddenly interested in the conversation. Previously, he was looking out of the limo window.

"He said, 'Shut your mouth! You went there?' and then I said, 'I stayed there all night long. The music was good!' "

"You a real Bajan, aren't you?" Shelly asks.

"I love it here," Mystique replies. "They'll speak in English for you at the resort, Sunday. I see you looking scared."

"Not scared, just wishing I had studied more on the dialect."

"Is that where we're staying?" Shelly asks as we pull into the drive for the Almond Casuarina Beach Resort.

Big D replies, "Yes. And we're going to shoot the video right on the beach."

Check-in is a breeze since Epsilon Records has paid for everything in full up front. I have a one-bedroom ocean-view suite and so do Big D and Shelly. Sam and Dilly are roommates, and Bethany is bunking with Regina, our makeup artist, in rooms with a garden view.

Since their rooms are not quite ready (we got in early),

Bethany, Sam, and Dilly come to my room to change into our bathing suits, so we can hit the beach for a little while. Dilly and I have to start makeup and hair for my video shoot in a few hours, because the first scene is a night shoot on the beach. One of the BET cameramen follows us. I know the filming is part of it, but his presence is somewhat annoying.

The bellhop opens the door to my room and I have to gasp with awe. I don't think I've ever stayed anywhere as nice as this! The sitting room—yes, sitting room—is decked out with tan and wicker furniture, and there is a patio with a table and chairs.

"Can we open that door?" I ask the bellhop.

"Yes, but be careful of de tree frogs. Dey might come in and sing fuh yuh."

I laugh out loud. "Tree frogs! Oh my goodness."

"Maybe you can open it when you get ready to go out there, and then close it behind you," Sam says. "I've seen you around insects—I don't think that would be a good look for the cameras to catch you running from a frog."

I smile over at Sam. He seems to be in a better mood than he was at the airport. I don't know if it's for the BET cameras or if it's the faint coconut scent in the island air. I mean, how could you not feel good with the breeze from the Caribbean Sea caressing your face? Poetic much? I know. . . . I can't help it. This place makes me want to be lyrical.

The bellhop gives a little bow as he backs out of the room. I run to my purse for a tip. My mother told me this before I left—"Everybody who touches your bags will want some money."

"Your room is banging!" Dilly says. "I hope ours is this nice."

Sam laughs out loud. "I'm sure it'll be nice, but it won't be this big."

Suddenly a little tired, I sprawl onto the comfortable sofa in my room. "Bethany, I didn't get to congratulate you on your record deal with Mystique. Is she planning on using any of me and Sam's music on your album?"

"I think so, but she also wants to use some other writers so that I have a different sound from you and Dreya."

"That makes sense, but I heard the finished copies of the tracks you did with me and Sam's songs. You sound really good."

"Thank you. And thanks for the congratulations too. I didn't know if you'd be happy about me signing on with Mystique too."

"Why wouldn't I be happy?" I ask. "I wasn't writing songs for you so that you *wouldn't* get a record deal."

"It's just that some people say that they want to help you, but then they just end up using you in the process."

She gets really quiet after saying this, which makes me think she's referring to Truth. I could've told her that he wouldn't help her get a record deal. I mean, really, how would he be able to do that with Dreya breathing down his neck. Truth and Dreya are completely obsessed with one another, so he would've never been able to keep his promises to Bethany.

"Well, some people are not me! I do what I say I'm gonna do."

Bethany plops down next to me on the couch. "This

room is nice! And you're staying in here all by your lone-some. Are you sure you don't want a roommate?"

I respond by lifting one eyebrow and smirking. On the surface, Bethany seems to be a different person from the one who hooked up with Romell, my ex-boyfriend, tried to hook up with Sam, and hooked up with Dreya's cur-rent boyfriend, Truth. But, her track record is way too bad for me to let her back in the friend circle that easily, even if I do want her to have a recording career.

Still, with Sam acting sometimey, I don't know if I really have a friend here in Barbados. Mystique doesn't count because she doesn't know how to let her hair down until Zac comes around. And I sure can't count Dreya, not with Truth in the mix.

"Let's get dressed, y'all. Mystique will be rounding me and Dilly up in a little bit, and I read in the brochure that they have snorkeling and kayaking."

"You trying to do all that?" Sam asks.

"One or the other right now, and then the rest after we get done shooting tomorrow."

Dilly smiles as he makes a dash toward the bedroom. "Guys get dressed first! Y'all take way too long."

I laugh out loud. Has this dude met me? I'm so not the primping and fussing girl that would take all day to get ready for the beach. He's got me confused with Dreya.

When it's me and Bethany's turn to get dressed in the bedroom, I take advantage of the fact that I have her alone.

"Bethany, are you okay with Truth being here?"

She takes a long pause before responding. "I'm not

gonna lie, it really shocked me that he showed up. He knows that Epsilon doesn't want him here, or they would've paid for it."

"Yeah, I'm tripping because he and Dreya are not even supposed to be back together. You know he badly sprained her ankle, right?"

Bethany's eyes get huge. "No, I didn't know that he did that. I thought they were so in love."

"I don't know what to call it, but it isn't love. I just want to make sure that you aren't still digging him. Dilly might get kind of twisted."

"I don't like him anymore. He was just playing me anyway. I wish I'd never fallen for his games."

"I'm just checking, because this reality show is supposed to be drama free. They'll probably just edit out all the stuff they don't want to show."

Bethany sighs as she checks out her reflection in the mirror. I know she can tell that her bikini is like two sizes too small, but I think she likes the effect of her butt cheeks hanging out all over the place. My mom would choke the life out of me if I was on TV looking like that.

In less than fifteen minutes, we emerge from the bedroom, ready for the beach. Sam and Dilly both are wearing long trunks and flip-flops. Both of them are ripped in the abdominal area. Six-packs all over the place. I guess musicians work out too.

I'm wearing a cute tankini with boy shorts. It's pink and green on top and white on the bottom. And both boys are appreciating Bethany's too small bikini. She starts putting that bodacious backside on display.

"Y'all look hot!" Dilly exclaims. "We might have to fight some Bajan dudes over them, Sam."

Sam chuckles. "Sunday is her own woman! If she wants to holla at a Bajan dude, who am I to stop her?"

I watch Dilly and Bethany exchange shocked glances. Sam gets on my nerves. I just roll my eyes at him and storm out of my suite. Oh well to the BET cameras getting all this on film. I'm too mad to worry about that right now.

As soon as I see the beach, my anger evaporates. I just can't stay angry in the face of so much beauty. I run across the white sand, leaving my friends in the dust.

When I get to the edge of the water, I don't stop, I just run right in! It's high noon, the sun is beaming down, and the water is warm!

"Dang, Sunday!" Sam gasps when he finally catches up to me. "You're like a mermaid or something! Just running to the water like it's home."

"I love the beach!" I say. "We hardly ever get to go back home."

Bethany sticks a toe in the water. "Girl, this is cold. I think I'll just sit myself on one of these beach chairs and get a tan."

Dilly runs into the water too. He actually starts swimming as soon as he gets in.

"You're a fish, boy! This water is kind of choppy," I say as he pops back up out of the water.

"This is nothing. Sam, you coming in?"

He shakes his head. "I'm about to go down there and see about the kayak rental. That's what you want to do, right, Sunday?"

I nod speechlessly. I don't know what to make of Sam today. He disses me at the airport and then flirts with a pretty Bajan girl as soon as we touch down. Now he's taking care of what I want to do? Something is not adding up.

"Are y'all a couple or not?" Dilly asks me after Sam leaves to get the kayak, mirroring the thoughts in my head.

"Not, I think. But I can't figure Sam out to save my life. One day he's crushing on me, the next he's telling me to kick rocks."

I didn't mean to be that candid to Dilly, but he's about as good as anyone right now. I really need to work on cultivating my friendships. Maybe Sam was onto something when he talked about me chasing dollars. If the only person I have to talk to is someone who hated me a couple weeks ago, then there is a serious problem.

A few moments later, Truth and Dreya get to the beach. Dreya stands at the edge of the water with her hands on her hips and legs spread akimbo looking like an R&B chick rendition of Wonder Woman.

"You could've told me y'all were coming to the beach," Dreya says.

I laugh out loud and slurp in a little salt water (eww). "Girl, stop. You know good and well that you and Truth don't want to hang out with us!"

"I want to be wherever the cameras are," Dreya says.

"I'm not worried about Bethany at all. Plus, she's got her little high school junior boyfriend with her. . . ."

"I'm a senior!" Dilly fusses as he sends a wall of water splashing in Dreya's direction. "A senior just like you."

Oooooh! No he didn't just bring up the fact that Dreya didn't graduate. That is a sore subject with her, and she doesn't like to talk about it.

"Whatever, Dilly. I just passed my summer-school English class with flying colors. My diploma is in the mail."

I walk out of the water and up to Dreya. "Why didn't you tell my mom, and Aunt Charlie?"

"Because I don't really feel like talking to them right now. Every conversation I have with my mother is about her telling me to stay away from Truth."

My eyes follow Truth as he heads over to the kayaks with Sam. "It's not without reason, Dreya. Aren't you concerned he's going to do something again? You aren't scared?"

"Listen, the times that he put his hands on me, I really, really made him mad. I'm just not going to do that anymore."

"Are you listening to yourself? You said you're not going to make him mad! That's impossible. There's no way you can be in a relationship with a person and not get them mad at you for something."

"All I have to do is love him unconditionally. He's the one for me, Sunday. Every day I see that more and more. I want to spend the rest of my life with him."

I shake my head sadly. Dreya reminds me of a song

that my mom loves to sing by Tina Turner, "A Fool in Love."

"Well, that's not going to happen if Aunt Charlie has anything to do with it."

"She doesn't run my life, Sunday. I'm grown."

Bethany strides past us and into the water with Dilly. She says something to him and then they both get out.

"I thought y'all were going kayaking with us," I say.

Bethany says, "Nah, we're going to the pool."

"You know what it is," Dilly adds.

I *know* they don't want to be out here with Truth and Dreya, but who does? Not me! Especially since Sam is acting all kinds of ridiculous.

"Well, I guess I'll see you for the video shoot then, Dilly."

He waves as he walks behind Bethany. "Okay, cool."

Dreya rolls her eyes. "Good riddance."

"Oh, for crying out loud, Dreya. Give it a rest. Everybody knows what Bethany and *Truth* did. If you can forgive him, at least you can act civil toward her."

"Nah, friends don't do what Bethany did. I'll never be cool with her again."

"I agree, what she did was awful, but I don't know if you two were ever friends to begin with. I mean, you treated her like the bottom of your shoe when she was your so-called assistant."

"I treated her the way you treat an assistant. She just didn't like the job."

Sam and Truth walk back up right before I give Dreya another jab. We're getting really used to these cameras being around, I think, because I'm speaking my mind like they're not even here.

Sam says, "You ready for your kayak ride? Where'd Dilly and Bethany go?"

"They left. Too much extra company."

Dreya narrows her eyes. "You know what? Truth and I can leave too."

"Girl, bye! Take the cameras with you if you want. It seems like that's the most important thing to you anyway."

"Why y'all always arguing?" Truth asks. "Can't we just get along for the next four days?

"Boy, please! You're not even supposed to be here!"

"Come on, babe. I saw a nice, quiet spot on the beach, farther down past the kayak rental shack," Truth says.

Dreya takes Truth's arm and walks away in the direction of the shack. She looks back like she's half waiting on the cameras to follow her. Okay, I was joking about that. They're not really going to follow her. I knew it and so did she.

"Are we going on the kayak?" Sam asks again, this time sounding a little annoyed.

"Only if you want to," I reply. "I'm not in the mood for anyone else's attitude."

Sam chuckles. "What about your attitude? Are you in the mood for your attitude?"

"Right. My attitude. Yeah, well, your people get on my nerves."

"Dem in nuh good," he replies.

I burst into laughter. "Sam, seriously! You too with the Bajan speak?"

"Yeah! I did my homework. Don't hate me because you didn't do yours."

"So what did you just say?"

"They are no good."

I nod in agreement. They are absolutely no good. "Let's go. The kayak is waiting!"

17

It's a good thing I'm already sun-kissed, because this sun is hot! I put on sunscreen too because Mystique fussed and told me to, and now I'm glad I did. Sitting out in the Caribbean Sea in a kayak with the sun beating down is no joke.

But still, it's beautiful.

I glance over the side of our kayak, which is now bobbing effortlessly over the waves. "Look, you can see fish in the water."

"I know. That's awesome, right?"

"Heck yeah. Dilly and Bethany are missing out."

Sam coughs and then clears his throat. "Maybe it's better that they didn't come out with us."

"What do you mean?"

"This is so relaxing, and they've got a lot of chatter. Bethany chatters nonstop and Dilly is likely to bust a freestyle at any given time. It's better that they're not here."

I totally flatline at "likely to bust a freestyle." This is funny because it is one-hundred-percent true. You can say hello to Dilly, and he asks you if you're favorite color is yellow and where you like to hang when you're mellow.

He's not a playa, he just raps a lot! OMG!

"You know this is the dream, right? You're living the dream," Sam says.

"We're living the dream."

Sam lifts his hands and motions wildly in the sky. "This is not my dream! My dream doesn't include reality shows and tours. My dream is me and my keyboard banging out hot beats."

"To be honest, all of this isn't my dream either, although I don't know what I thought was going to happen with our singing group. I mean, I like being on stage and performing, but I really just want to go to college and be a regular girl."

"You are going to college, but you dang sure aren't going to be regular when you get there."

"I know! I don't want to be the celeb on campus. I won't even be able to go to a fraternity party without it showing up on Mediatakeout.com."

"Wow . . . you planning to go to frat parties? I thought you were going to college to learn."

I laugh out loud. "Shut up! I'm going for the whole experience. The parties, the step shows, the lectures. I want all of it."

"And have it you shall. Under the ever-watchful eyes of Atlanta's bloggers."

I glance off into the distance, at a splash in the water. "What kind of fish is making all that ruckus?"

Sam's eyes widen. "That's not a fish, Sunday. That's a person! A girl is in the water!"

I squint to see better, since my vision is partially obstructed by the sun. It is a girl, and she's flailing her arms, trying to yell and dipping beneath the surface of the water.

"Help!" I scream as if someone can hear me. We're about two hundred feet from the shore, but it might as well be a thousand.

"She's not that far from us, maybe fifty yards," Sam says. "I'm gonna try to get her."

"You're not supposed to do that! Someone who is drowning will pull the other person under! They taught us that in swimming class."

"But I'm trained as a lifeguard, and I'm a strong swimmer. Just stay here, I'm gonna pull her back to the kayak."

I'm screaming my head off as Sam jumps in the water and swims toward the drowning girl. I wave my hands in the air and holler, pretty sure I look like an imbecile to anyone standing on the beach.

A lady looks at me and waves back. Then she runs toward the kayak shack. She sees me!

Sam finally gets to the girl, and she pulls him under more than once before he can get his arms around her. When she finally relaxes, he starts to pull her back to the kayak. I can see the vein on his forehead throbbing as he struggles to pull the girl.

He gets to the kayak and throws one arm over the side. Then he props the girl against the side of the kayak. It looks uncomfortable, but there's no way that he can get the girl in the boat without tipping the thing over.

"Row, Sunday. Row us back to shore."

"By myself? I'm not strong enough."

"Yes, you are. The water will help. It's only two hundred feet."

I struggle with the oars that are connected to the kayak, but finally I get them going in the correct direction and we're moving. Slowly, but we are moving. The girl is barely breathing; she's probably swallowed too much water.

When I'm almost to the shore, several men run into the water and pull us the rest of the way. Why am I angry that the BET cameras are filming all of this? I can't believe we're having a near-death experience, and they're videotaping it.

"My baby!" the lady screamed.

The men take the girl and gingerly place her on the beach. Another woman starts CPR, and after a few one one thousand, two one thousands, the girl sputters water everywhere, and starts to cry.

The girl's mother (I presume) runs up to Sam and hugs him around his neck. He stumbles back a few steps. He's probably not too strong himself after his daring rescue.

"You saved my daughter's life, young man. I owe you everything."

Sam shakes his head. "You don't owe me. I would've done it for anyone. I'm just glad Sunday, here, dragged me kayaking."

The lady hugs me too. "God bless both of you. If it weren't for you my daughter would've drowned."

I feel a twinge of guilt in my midsection because I had tried to talk Sam out of rescuing her, but no one has to hear that!

"Sunday, if you don't mind, I want to go back to the hotel and lie down. I'm suddenly very tired."

"Wait. Let me ask the medic." I don't like how wobbly Sam looks.

I run up to the medic as his crew gets the young girl on a stretcher. "Does he need oxygen or something?" I ask. "He doesn't look too well."

The medic trots over to Sam and makes him sit down on the sand. He checks Sam's pulse and his other vital signs. He motions for someone to bring him an oxygen mask, tank, and some water.

"Take a few deep breaths on this," the medic says.

Sam obeys, and the grayish cast that his skin had taken gives way to his normal golden glow. He closes his eyes as he inhales like it's the breath of life or something.

"Stay here and rest for a few moments, but under a shade umbrella. Then when you're feeling a little bit stronger go indoors and rest. Both of you." The medic looks at me as well.

"I'm fine," I reply. "Why do I need to rest?"

"The amount of adrenaline it took for you to row that kayak quickly back to shore will drain you of all your energy. You need to take a nap before you participate in any more activities."

I nod thoughtfully. This makes sense, of course, but to hear it come from a medic as if it's an order makes it sound a bit more serious.

I sit down next to Sam in the sand. "Are you okay?" I

ask. "Let me know when you're ready to go back to the rooms."

"Give me a minute, okay?"

I dig my feet into the sand and whisper to Sam. "You're a hero, dude!"

He smiles, but doesn't reply. I wonder what it feels like to know that you just saved someone's life. If it wasn't for Sam feeling brave today, that girl would have drowned. She can't be more than thirteen.

That's deep.

We sit for what seems like a long while, enjoying the sea breeze and watching the crowd thin out. After the girl gets taken away in the ambulance/taxi, there isn't much more excitement.

"I think I'm ready now," Sam says.

"Okay, black Superman, let's hustle back to the resort, before Mystique's head explodes."

"I forgot you have to get ready for your video shoot," Sam says as he stands. "I'm sorry."

"It's cool. You were too busy saving lives!"

Sam gives me a huge smile that literally takes my breath away. If the resort's medic sees me anytime soon, he's gonna hit me with a one one thousand, two one thousand, for real. Then, he might just put that oxygen mask on my face!

"You okay, Sunday?" Sam asks.

"I'm perfect, Sam."

Absolutely perfect.

18

"Tell me about the rescue."

The BET cameraman and producer thought it would be best for me to do a confessional about Sam rescuing the girl almost as soon as we got back to the hotel. I got into hair and makeup for the first scene with Dilly and they were right outside the room waiting for me.

I shift on the tiny stool and try to get comfortable. I think they purposely pick these stools, because the only thing you can do is sit straight up, and look like you've got incredibly great posture when you would really rather slump.

"The rescue was awesome. Sam was . . . he was incredible. I've never seen anything so brave."

"Was there any point in time that you were afraid? Did you think Sam wouldn't make it back to the kayak?"

I pause for a moment to collect my thoughts. "I was afraid, but I can't say that there was enough time to think or analyze the situation. Sam jumped in the water and I think we both just kind of went on autopilot after that."

"Does Sam's bravery make you want him as a boyfriend?"

OMG! Seriously? I didn't think they'd go here, but of course, I should've known. They love to go here. It's what gives them an interesting show.

"I don't really like to talk about my personal life, but I did admire what Sam did out there. I will definitely say that."

"Okay, thanks, Sunday," the producer says.

When I walk out of the confessional room, Mystique is pacing up and down the resort hallway looking really twisted. The director of my music video, Lena Che, is here too and she doesn't look happy either.

"What's going on?" I ask. "You don't like my hair or something?"

Mystique looks up and appraises me as if she hadn't already done it. Ooookay. It definitely wasn't my hair that's the problem. She just keeps pacing.

Lena says in her clipped British accent, "Sunday, it looks as if we'll have to postpone the shooting."

"Postpone? Why? We're only here a few days!" I would hate for them to not get the footage they need, and me end up having a bootleg video that we film outside of Big D's studio.

"Because Dilly went and got sunburned," Mystique says. "I told that high-yellow dummy to put on some sunscreen."

"Wait a minute, can't we just cover it up with makeup? I mean isn't sunburn just a little redness?"

Mystique shakes her head. "He didn't just burn his skin, he basically got sun poisoning. He and Bethany were out by the pool at high noon with no shade at all. He's got a fever, chills, and vomiting."

"You have got to be kidding me!" I say. "What's the contingency plan?"

Lena and Mystique look at one another, but neither of them respond.

"You mean to tell me that we came all the way to Barbados, and we don't have a backup plan for this type of thing?" I hear myself ranting, and I try to calm myself down.

Lena replies, "I do know of a modeling agency in Bridgetown that can probably get us someone acceptable, but I don't know if we can get them today. It's Friday afternoon, and everyone is getting prepped for their weekend jobs. The models left will probably not be who you want to use."

"Well, see about it anyway," Mystique says. "In the meantime, I need you to practice your moves so that you can help whoever we hire. Lord knows they're not going to have enough time to learn any choreography."

"You want me to practice by myself? I don't know if that's gonna be effective," I say, and I'm being one-hundred-percent honest. I need a practice partner.

"Maybe if Sam's head has shrunk back down to normal size, he can help you," Mystique chuckles.

I didn't think Sam had a big head about the rescue at all. He answered all of the questions everyone asked, with grace and patience. Even when they asked the same question several times. I heard someone mumble that they thought it was staged for the BET camera that was just so conveniently following us on the beach. That irked me, but Sam didn't even flinch and he was close enough to hear it too.

"Sam will help. I just have to ask him."

Lena asks, "Why can't we use the other guy? The rapper that came with Drama? He might be better than a model."

"No way," Mystique replies. "Epsilon would trip all the way out if we had Truth in that video. They don't want Sunday attached to him at all. He's not even supposed to be here."

Lena shrugs. "Well, then, I'm off to make some phone calls. I'll be back to help with the practicing."

"Make it happen!" Mystique calls after her.

Instead of going all the way back to the suites, I call Sam's cell phone.

"Hello?" He sounds like he's still sleeping.

"Sam, are you up?"

"I am now. What's good?"

"We kind of had an emergency. Dilly can't be in the video. . . . He's sick."

"Mmmkay . . ."

I want to burst out laughing. I know Sam so well. And he's thinking, *What does this have to do with me?*

"So can you just help me practice while we wait on the replacement to show up?"

I can hear Sam's sigh of relief over the phone. "Oh, is that all? Okay, yeah I can do that."

"What? Did you think I was gonna make you learn some choreography or something?"

Sam laughs. "You know I don't dance."

"Real men dance."

"Real men stand on the wall, while girls back it up!"

I crack up. "Whatever, boy. Can you just get down to the beach cabana? Mystique wants to try to get some practice in since I've got on all this hair and makeup."

"Okay. See you in a few."

I press End on the phone and notice that Mystique is staring at me.

"What?"

She gives me a sly grin. "Is someone's on-again, off-again relationship back on again?"

"Um . . . no. Not that I know of. Sam has been pretty clear that he's sick of me playing games and chasing money."

"But you were cheesing hard just now when you were talking to him."

And now, I'm cheesing again. "Well, I never said anything about my crush dissipating. He's the one that's done with me."

"I see. Well let's go to the cabana and wait for him."

It's crazy going anywhere with Mystique. Even walking from the hotel to the cabana house is a flurry of autographs and pictures with fans. She handles it well, though. She never looks irritated and always has a smile for a little girl or teenager who shouts, "I love you, Mystique!" I even sign a couple of autographs too. It doesn't bother me one bit that some of the kids had no idea who I am. It's okay. They will.

When we get to the cabana house, there is a huge

group of Bajan teenagers wearing assorted bathing suits. They're all getting hair and makeup for the video.

"Why couldn't we just use one of them?" I ask. "A couple of them look *quite* acceptable."

"Because if it's not going to be Dilly, it can't just be some random dude. There are a few models that are *really* hot. Not just regular-guy hot."

"I like regular guys," I protest.

"I know. That is a problem," Mystique replies.

I toss my head back and snort. "What's wrong with regular guys?"

"Regular guys don't get us! They don't get the music industry. They don't get the drive that it takes to get and remain on top. That's why Sam is so frustrated with you."

I sigh and nod. "Because he wants me to do regular-chick things."

"Right, like getting your nails done, arguing with him for looking at another girl, or texting him all night."

"It's not that I wouldn't or don't do all of those things," I say.

"Right, but first and foremost, what is it?"

"It's the music, it's the money. For college, for my mama. You know what it is."

"Believe me, I know. I tried to date regular guys. I even tried to have regular girlfriends and it didn't work. My regular boyfriends were always jealous and the girls get jealous too at some point."

"So that's how you ended up with Zac?" I ask.

"Yep. Zac understands the grind. He understands

everything I do to be successful. And he's not threatened by it. He loves me more for it. My grind complements his hustle."

I give serious thought to this as Dreya walks up wearing an almost invisible flesh-colored two-piece bikini. Is Sam always going to feel like second fiddle to my music career? And is he going to be able to handle anything else I do?

Can I not deal with the regular?

On closer inspection, I can see that Dreya got her hair and makeup done too. This girl was not playing when she said she was going to be wherever the cameras are. Mystique takes one look at her and rolls her eyes.

"Hey, cuzzo," Dreya says. "You look fly."

Since getting a compliment from Dreya is a rarity, I reply, "Thank you, cuzzo. You look good too."

Then I realize that she probably only gave me a compliment so that the cameras could catch her being benevolent to her cousin. . . . Wow. . . .

"So, I thought you and Truth would be hanging at the beach or something."

She shrugs and looks away from me. "Nah. I don't know where he is. Probably kicking it with Sam and Big D or something."

"Sam's here. He's about to come down to practice with me, but maybe he's with Big D. I haven't seen Big D since we checked in."

"I think Big D and Shelly had a couples' spa day," Mystique says.

I chuckle at the thought of Big D getting a pedicure, or

a hot rocks massage. Ha! Shelly deserves it, though. She puts up with much mess from Big D and from all of his artists.

Dreya's facial expression is strange. It's her thinking pose, but she's also got a fake smile plastered on her face. I know what the smile is for—the camera—but what is she thinking about?

Just when I decide to ask her, Sam strides across the beach looking well rested. He smiles like he's excited to practice for a video shoot when I know he's really not that excited.

"So what do y'all want me to do?" Sam asks. "Stand where dude is gonna stand so Sunday can do her thang?"

Mystique replies, "A little more than stand there. I need you to at least walk through, so she can get her musical queues down."

"At least walk through?" Sam asks. "If that's the least I can do, what's the most I can do?"

I laugh out loud. "You feeling real frisky, aren't you?"

Mystique joins in with my laughter. "Okay, Sam. You can do the choreography too if you want."

"Let me see it," Sam says.

"Didn't you just say men don't dance?" I ask.

"Well, I'm not about to do any *crazy* dancing, but maybe a couple of steps."

Mystique says, "Welll, there's not really a lot of dancing. Sunday is going to see you at a beach party. You're posted up on the side sipping a beverage, but your eyes meet."

"That's on the first verse, right?" I ask.

"Yes," Mystique nods. "When you're singing *When I first saw you/You were so incredible to me/All I could do is watch you/A guy like you would never talk to me.*"

"That doesn't sound hard," Sam says.

"Then on the bridge where she says, *Seems like I'm hiding in plain sight/Wish you would open up your eyes,* you're going to walk toward her like you are coming up to talk to her, but you're going to walk through her like she's invisible. That part we'll do with a green screen."

Sam claps his hands together. "That's hot right there."

"It is," Mystique agrees. "I just wish Dilly wasn't sick. We've already practiced it with him."

"I can do it," Sam says.

"Show and prove," Mystique says.

Lena, the video director, walks up to us. She had been coaching the group of extras and now she probably wants to show Sam the ropes.

"Drama, exactly where do you plan to be while we're shooting?" Lena asks. "I need to make sure you don't contaminate any of my shots."

Dreya's face scrunches into an angry frown. "What do you mean contaminate your shot? If you get me in it, you've done nothing but upgrade your shot."

Lena rolls her eyes and looks at Mystique. Mystique rubs the back of her own neck as if stressed and then sighs.

"Drama," she says slowly and deliberately, "can you please make sure that you are not in any of the video shots? I would, and Epsilon would, greatly appreciate it if we didn't have to do extra filming because of you."

"Aren't y'all just practicing right now anyway?" Dreya

asks. "Sam's not going to be in the final video. So why do I have to worry about getting out of the way?"

"Because," Lena explains, "if I get any usable footage, I'm using it. Actually, I like the look of Sam. Let's get him in makeup before we shoot, just in case I want to keep him."

"But he's not a leading-man type," Mystique argues. "He's just a round-the-way kind of regular guy."

Lena shrugs and smiles. "Sometimes regular works. My first four husbands were regular guys."

I lift my eyebrows at Mystique and grin. Sometimes regular works, even if you are a superstar, all about your business.

Lena jogs over to the extras to give some final orders, and Mystique whispers, "Her first four husbands . . . where are those regular guys now?"

"For real, y'all are not gonna let me be in this video?" Dreya asks. "Y'all are tripping."

"Is that what you want? To be an extra in Sunday's video?" Mystique asks. "I thought you were too much of a star for that."

"An *extra*? Puh-lease. I don't want to be an extra. I want to play a starring role in the video. Like on that first part you're talking about where Sunday first makes eye contact with Sam, she and I could be having a conversation."

"What?" Mystique asks.

"Then when she finally gets his attention, I can introduce them." Dreya looks one-hundred-percent proud of herself and her idea, and I'm just about sure that Mystique is voting no.

"The whole point of the video," Mystique says, "is that Sunday is an apparition that he can't see."

"An apparition?" Dreya asks. "What's that?"

OMG! Hooked on Phonics Dreya.

"It's like a ghost," Mystique says.

"Oh . . . oh! Well, that's just stupid," Dreya says after I think the lightbulb clicks on for her.

Mystique replies, "It's not stupid, but there is no room for Sunday to interact with anyone, except Sam at the end when she materializes in his arms."

"Oh."

"So can you please," Mystique asks, "make yourself scarce? Why don't you go to the spa? Get yourself a spa pedicure on me or something."

"On you?" Dreya asks. "Can I get a full-body rock massage too?"

Mystique rolls her eyes. "Go ahead, Drama."

"All right, I'm out. And Sunday?"

"Yeah?" I ask.

"Don't even think about being in my next video, since you tripping so hard on your little debut."

I almost respond, but then decide it's not worth it. It kills me how she always tries to blame me for someone else's decision. Epsilon and Lena decided what this video was going to be like. I guess I'm the easiest one to blame for everything because she knows that I'm always gonna be her cousin no matter what.

Lena jogs back over to us. "Okay, I'm ready to film the first scene. You should be lip-synching to your lyrics. You can even sing them if it helps you stay in time with the music. We're going to dub in the sound anyway, so it doesn't matter what you do vocally."

"So we're doing the first verse?" I ask.

"Yes. We're going to do the first verse now, but we'll go through the whole song several times, so I can have different shots of you. Some we're going to do with you lying on the sand. Some we're gonna have with you dancing on the shore. You're gonna get sick of the verses to this song."

"Okay, let's make it happen," Mystique says.

I'm mildly more conscious of the BET cameras than the ones that Lena brought for the video shoot. It seems like they're there to catch my simplest mistake or slip on judgment.

Everyone takes their places, and when Lena says, "Action," it's on and poppin'! I'm surprised at how many of the queues, movements, and dances I remember from our practices in Atlanta.

It feels weird singing the lyrics of my song toward Sam. I've never been invisible to him. He's seen me from the jump. I can't say that I saw him immediately, but after we vibed on the music, I *did* see him, and wondered what a relationship with him might be like. It scared me, so I looked away. It was easier to look at my music career than look at him.

But now that I'm cool with seeing him, even if it's through a squinted side eye, I can't get him to pay me any attention. Some people would call that ironic; I call it me getting what I deserve.

We walk through these scenes for hours. So long, in

fact, that I have to stop in the middle and get my hair and makeup refreshed, because I sweated out my hair and streaked my mascara.

Finally, the extras are getting a rest, because we're filming the scene where I end up in Sam's arms. Lena starts the shooting and then abruptly stops it. She walks over to us, so that she can place our bodies correctly for the cameras.

"Why are you two standing so far apart?" Lena says. "I need to feel your tension through the lens."

There's tension all right. Sam keeps staring at me like he's Robinson Crusoe seeing a steak the first time after he's rescued from that deserted island.

Sam grins and pulls me in close, like he was just waiting on the opportunity to do that.

"Perfect!" Lena says. "Keep that intensity."

She starts filming again. Then she stops. Again.

"Sunday! Don't forget to lip-synch!"

Dang, Sam's got me totally mesmerized to the point where I forgot my song lyrics. I tried to lip-synch, but I couldn't even get it together. I think Sam can tell how twisted I am, because he hasn't wiped that grin off his face yet.

Lena starts filming again. Then she stops. AGAIN!

"Good, Sunday, but Sam, I want you to tip her chin up with your hand, then gaze into her eyes, like you're just now noticing how beautiful her eyes are."

Sam does what he's told, and tips my chin up. He also does something she didn't tell him to do. He licks his lips like someone just handed him a bottle of A1 sauce.

Even though Lena hasn't directed him to do this, Sam

places a light kiss on my lips, then eases back and smiles. Is this real or for the cameras? If it's fake, then I need a reality check for real.

Lena squeals as she calls "Cut!" to her cameramen.

"Sam, man, you rock!" Lena says. "That kiss was perfection. I might want to use you for some of my other videos."

This immediately annoys me. If Sam can bring intensity like this to another girl, he and I will have some serious issues.

Mystique still looks skeptical, however. "I don't think that kiss needs to be in there. Everyone knows who Sam is from the reality show. I don't want Sunday's teenage-boy fans to think she's taken now. And that's exactly what they're gonna think if we show the footage of the two of them kissing."

Lena frowns deeply. "It's hot. I'm keeping it. I think the suits at Epsilon will love it too, not to mention Sunday's fans—boys and girls."

"I'm the one signing the checks on this one, Lena. It's for my label, remember?"

"Look, don't hire me if you're gonna screw with my artistry, Mystique."

Mystique flips a piece of her blond wig over her shoulder. "You were *hired* to bring my vision to life on this video."

Lena looks hurt by this. She clutches her midsection like Mystique just punched her and knocked the wind out of her.

"I cannot believe you, Mystique. After all the projects we've done . . ."

"All the projects I've paid for. Don't get it twisted, Lena."

Of course, the BET cameras are getting all this divatastic footage. From the way Mystique is throwing her weight around, I think she's doing it on purpose and for the cameras.

"How about you do two versions of the video and let the fans decide?" I ask.

Immediately, I wish I could take this back because it sounds totally scripted. Like something dreamed up in a producer's meeting at BET. But I'm really just trying to end this back-and-forth between Lena and Mystique and distract the cameras from the drama.

"Like a promotion for the album? That is a wonderful idea," Mystique says.

"That's gonna be a lot of work," Lena says.

Mystique sucks her teeth and rolls her eyes to the top of her head. "Lena, stop being a drama queen. You've got the raw footage, so just do it."

"Am I being paid for two edits? Because that's what this is . . . two edits."

"Yes! You know I'm good for it," Mystique replies.

Lena nods, and directs her film crew to start packing up. Then she turns to me. "Sunday, don't get wasted or anything tonight, in case we have to shoot anything else tomorrow."

Wasted as in drizzy-drunk? Puh-lease! Has she met me?

"Never that, Lena. I think we might go dancing at a reggae spot later, but I shan't be getting wasted. I don't roll like that."

Sam laughs and pulls me away from the set to another part of the beach that's a safe distance from the BET cameras. By the time we're out of recording range, Sam is cracking up and holding his midsection like someone just told him the funniest knock-knock joke in the history of knock-knocks.

"What is so funny?" I ask.

I have to wait while Sam finishes laughing, but when he finally composes himself he says, "I *shan't* be getting wasted? Sunday, you are funny. Was that your TV speak?"

"Do shut up! It wasn't that funny! OMG. I can't believe that's what you were laughing about. You are a butt."

"Or am I a hindquarter?" Sam says before erupting into another flurry of giggles.

Sam's laughter is contagious because even though it's at my expense, I'm laughing too. Hindquarter? Get the heck outta here.

"Did you mind?" Sam asks as he chokes out his last laughs.

"Did I mind what?"

"Me kissing you on the video shoot?"

I inhale deeply before answering. I know that my response to this question can make or break any chance at a relationship with Sam. If the kiss was Sam making a move, and I rebuff him, I think it's over. In fact, I *know* it's over. I don't even have to think twice about it.

But I don't know why he kissed me. What if he was just coming down off the adrenaline rush from saving the girl from drowning? Or worse, what if he just thought it would be good for the video? What if it wasn't a move at all?

"I didn't mind. . . . But did you mean it?" I ask.

Sam kicks a foot full of sand into the pretty, transparent, blue water. "I was afraid. . . ."

"Of kissing me?"

Sam shakes his head. "No. I mean when I saved the girl. Once I jumped in the water I got really scared, and started doubting myself a little bit. Then when I got to the girl and she pulled me under, I got even more scared, but while I was fighting to make it and swallowing water, I only thought about one thing."

"What was that?"

Sam clears his throat. "I just kept thinking how if I made it through this alive, that I was gonna make you my girlfriend, no matter what, and that I was gonna kiss you at the first real opportunity I got."

I'm speechless, and I have to look away from Sam. The intensity of his gaze is too much for me when I'm trying to figure out what to say to all this.

But it was the drowning incident that brought all this on, and I was afraid of that. What if he doesn't feel the same way after we get back home?

"Sunday . . . what's wrong?" Sam asks in a quivering voice.

"What if . . . what if it's just the adrenaline talking?"

Sam shakes his head. "This is me talking, and I'm saying the same thing I've been saying for the past six months."

I swallow hard, believing every single emotional syllable that comes from Sam's lips. His chest heaves up and down as if to provide a body-language exclamation mark to the end of his sentence.

And so I don't respond. Not with words. I put both arms around Sam's neck, hug him tight . . . and . . . kiss. Him. Back.

19

Hours after the video shoot, me, Sam, Dilly, and Bethany chill in my suite. We're trying to decide what's up for our first evening in Barbados. The ever-present BET cameraman is here too. I think he's trying to blend in with the scenery with his palm tree–covered Hawaiian shirt. But we still know he's there, and I can't speak for everyone else, but I'm extremely careful with what I say and how it can be construed as something else.

Bethany's brought all of her bags to my room, because she's going to get changed in here if we decide to go out. I think she's trying to move in for the weekend, but I don't know how I feel about that.

While I've taken Bethany out of enemy status, it's hard to think of her in the "friend" category anymore. Even if she seems okay. Even if she's got her own boyfriend and isn't trying to take anyone else's.

"Can you even go anywhere?" I ask Dilly.

"I don't know. I feel a lot better now. The burns still hurt though, so I should probably stay in."

"If you're staying in, then I am too," Bethany says as she puts yet another cool facecloth on Dilly's forehead. "I feel like it's my fault anyway that you're sick."

"It's not your fault I didn't put on sunscreen. Zac is gonna rip me a new one when he gets here. Y'all know this video was supposed to put me on the map."

Ouch! I didn't think about that when we haphazardly put Sam in Dilly's place. Maybe I should've tried to talk Mystique into delaying the video shoot until Dilly was better.

"Well, you're still here with us in Barbados," I say. "That's cool, right?"

"Yeah, it's cool, but I need my record to come out."

Bethany says, "Well, I just inked a deal with Mystical Sounds, so you should be in my first video. You're my boyfriend anyway, so that makes more sense."

Sam and I share a glance, and I know he's thinking what I'm thinking. Bethany signing a deal, having an album release and a video before Dilly is like rubbing salt in the wound. He'd been signed to Zac's label for over a year with no release date in sight.

"Speaking of your album, Bethany, I thought of a tight hook for you," I say. "It's an up-tempo track that could be a club banger. Good for a first single."

Sam says, "You talking about 'Get Like Me'?"

I nod and start singing, *"Get like me, get like me/My sound is like honey to a bee/Swagger drops you to your knees/Get like me, get like me."*

The hook is melodic and infectious. This is not me feeling myself, this is everybody bobbing their heads without a track. This is them feeling the melody and the lyrics and the flow. Hotness personified.

Captured by BET cameras. And you know this!

Bethany says, "I like that, Sunday! How do you do it? How do you keep coming up with song after song?"

"I don't know! I just hope it doesn't run out anytime soon."

"It won't," Sam says. "I think you've still got a lot of music inside of you. You're destined to be an icon."

"Icon! When I think of icons, I think of someone like Mystique," I say. "Someone who's been tried and tested in the game."

"Way to pay homage!" Dilly says.

I laugh out loud. "Is that what I'm doing? Paying homage?"

"Yeah," Sam replies. "A lot of artists refuse to acknowledge the ones who came before them and paved the way. But you're the real deal, so you don't have a problem with giving credit where credit is due."

"Real talk," I say. "So . . . what are we gonna do if we don't go out?"

Bethany grins. "Who said y'all had to stay in, just because we are?"

"Honestly, with everything that happened today, I have to admit I'm super exhausted," Sam says. "I'd probably be a boring date tonight."

"Yeah, me too. Let's get some room service and hang out," I say.

Bethany's eyes light up. "Y'all just gonna hang in the room all night with us?"

I refuse to make eye contact with Bethany when she's looking all hopeful like that. This doesn't have to mean that we're friends again. It just means that I don't hate her anymore. Forgiving somebody isn't something that just happens in an instant, and there's a whole lot of history that Bethany and I have to get past before we can be friends again.

But I'm not ruling it out.

"Um . . . I have no idea what the stuff is on this menu," Sam says, while holding up the room-service menu. "Who's feeling adventurous?"

I laugh out loud. "Give it to me. Let me see."

Sam gives me the menu and I read out loud. "Okay . . . roti. That is spiced meat rolled in a piece of flat bread called chapati. And conkies are cooked in banana leaves."

"I am not eating anything called a conkie," Dilly says.

"Open your mind! It's got cornmeal, pumpkin, raisins, spices, and a bunch of other stuff."

Bethany scrunches up her nose. "Have you ever tried it?"

"Um . . . no . . . but it sounds tasty."

"I wonder if there's a Pizza Hut in St. Lawrence Gap," Sam says.

"Y'all are tripping! I did not come all the way to Barbados for pizza!" I yell at the top of my lungs.

All three of them give me blank stares. Whatever!

"All right. Let's eat some rodeos and conned feet for Sunday," Sam says.

"That's *roti* and *conkies*. You all can bite me," I say as Sam picks up the phone to dial our order in.

"It better be good, Sunday," Dilly says. "I'm not well and I need something that tastes good to heal my body."

"I thought Dreya was the only drama queen in this crew!" I say.

With the food order placed, I plop down on one of the double beds in my room. Dilly is resting on the other one. The soft pillows and fluffy down comforter are welcoming. I didn't realize I was this tired. Who knew saving lives and filming videos would be this exhausting?

But then, I look at the BET camera dude and he just checked his watch like he's super bored and can't wait to get the heck out of here. Well, that just won't do. I can't have the cameraman thinking I'm boring. I am trying to have a hit show even if I don't ever want to do the whole reality thing again.

Then, I have an idea.

"I know what we can do, y'all. It'll be fun."

Sam claps his hands in a frantic and over-the-top manner. I know he's teasing me, and for that he gets the narrow-eyed glare.

"Anyway! Y'all can help me answer that fan letter I got. From the girl named Zoey."

Bethany says, "Okay, let's do this. Did you bring the letter?"

"Yep." I pull it out of the pocket of my purse.

"Didn't she say her boyfriend broke up with her on Facebook?" Sam asks.

I nod. "Yes, she says she logged on and his status was single. And that 'Can U See Me' helped her out when she was feeling sad. I've got to reach out to her."

Dilly laughs. "You're such a bleeding heart, Sunday."

"Whatever, hater. You'll do the same thing when you get some fan mail."

Bethany says, "I can't wait to get fan mail!"

"So help me write her back!"

Sam says, "Dear Zoey. Your boyfriend was a tool. You are better off without him. Thanks for purchasing my album and not bootlegging it. Ta ta for now. Sundeezy!"

I throw a pillow at Sam as he ducks and giggles.

"I was thinking something more like this. Dear Zoey, I'm so sad that your boyfriend played you like that. But love can be really rough sometimes. Sometimes it doesn't work out, but there's always another fish in the sea."

Dilly shakes his head. "Boring. Tell her that her new boo is right around the corner."

I write that down. That is a decent suggestion.

"And tell her," Dilly continues, "that another boy's trash is another one's wifey."

I scrunch my nose this time.

"Too much?" Dilly asks.

Bethany says, "Tell her that her ex-boyfriend was just there to pass the time until the boy of her dreams could come along. When he comes, she'll know it and there won't be any doubt."

Dilly, Sam, and I stare at Bethany. She seems to have gone to some other fairy-tale, romance-novel place. I'ma need her to come back. Earth calling Bethany . . .

"Okay, I'll use some of that too, Bethany. But you got stars in your eyes, boo. Somebody got you sprung!"

Bethany blushes, and so does Dilly. No wait, Dilly is badly sunburned, I can't tell if he's blushing or not. But he's got that "I-got-game" cheesy grin on lock.

I clear my throat and hold my hotel stationery up. "This is what I've got so far. Dear Zoey. It really blows that your boyfriend would break up with you on Facebook, but your new boo is right around the corner. Your ex-boyfriend was not the guy for you and he was just there to pass the time until the boy of your dreams comes along. Breaking up is hard, but it's not the end of the world. So chill and enjoy being a hot girl! Thanks for buying my music! Much love, Sunday."

"That's good," Sam says. "What it lacks in finesse it makes up for in raw honesty."

"What it *lacks* in finesse?" I launch another pillow at Sam.

"I'm joking, I'm joking. It's a good letter," Sam says.

Bethany snuggles in closer to Dilly on the bed.

"Um . . . ain't no freakiness about to take place in my room," I say. "Y'all getting a bit too cozy on that bed."

Bethany deserts Dilly and plops her inflated behind down at the end of my bed. "Is this better?" she asks.

"It'll do for now. How's it going with Regina? She's a cool roommate, right?" I ask.

Bethany nods. "Yeah, she's great, but she's like ten years older than us, so we really don't have much to talk about."

This is, I guess, the time when I'm supposed to invite her to stay in my room. She's giving me a sad puppy-dog face. Then, her cell phone buzzes in her pocket and she jumps as if it startles her.

"Are you going to check that?" Dilly asks.

"Um . . . no. I'm straight," Bethany replies. "Everybody I want to talk to is right here."

The silence in the room is so thick and heavy, it's like someone dropped a bag of wet sand in the middle of the floor.

Bethany being all secretive makes me happy that I didn't put her back in the friend box. Obviously, she's still on some mess, or she would've just answered the text. I'm sending her mental signals to just open the text message! Read it aloud or something. Anything to let everybody in this room know that she is not shady anymore, and that she's worthy of Dilly's ever-growing crush.

But Bethany does nothing but stare at the chipped polish on her nails.

So much for turning over a new leaf.

20

You have got to be kidding me! I knew that Dreya was going to pull something ridiculous with her and Truth's so-called plan, but this is just . . . well, Dreya is just out of control.

After we ate dinner, Sam pulled out his laptop and opened up Sandrarose.com. I wish he hadn't, because the spicy Bajan food is now turning in my stomach.

Sam reads, *"Epsilon Records artists and first cousins Drama and Sunday Tolliver are beefing again on the verge of Sunday's album release. Drama reached out to us personally about the reality show that they filmed for their summer tour. The show debuts tonight on BET. This is what Drama had to say to her fans: 'Everything you'll see on the show is completely edited beyond recognition. Mystique and her mother . . . well . . . they all have a vested interest in seeing Sunday blow up, so they* turned a show that was supposed to be about my come-up into something that's all about Sunday. I'm never gonna hate on my cousin, because that's blood. And I want everyone to go out and buy Sunday's album—if you like that Disney pop sound. She's a sweet girl, but I'm hot. Heat always rises to the top.' Sounds like a battle in the making! My snitches tell me that the whole Epsilon Records crew is on their way to Barbados to film a video for Sunday's single 'Can U See Me.' With leading man, and high school senior Dilly, maybe Drama isn't too far off with the Disney assessment. Only time and record sales will tell!'"

"Is that all of it?" I ask Sam.

He nods. "But it looks like she gave similar interviews to Bossip.com, Theybf.com, and Mediatakeout.com."

Dilly, now sitting up on the sofa with Bethany next to his feet, says, "She's foul. Just foul. I know she's just trying to keep her name in print, but dang, you don't nuke your own blood."

"Exactly!" Sam says. "She's only here because you begged Epsilon to let her come and she's gonna play you out like that?"

I shake my head and pace the sitting room. "I don't know why she would try to mess up my album release. I would *never* do that to her."

Bethany says, "I think you should stop being stupid, Sunday. Just confront her. What's she gonna do?"

I take out my cell phone and call Dreya.

"What's up, Sunday?" she says.

"Can you come to my room? I need to talk to you about something."

"Yeah," she says, and then hangs up.

"Sam," I say, "can you get the BET video guy back in here? We're about to settle this for once and for all. She wants to call me out on the blogs? Well, I'm gonna call her out on TV. It's about to be on."

A few minutes later, the BET cameraman is back in the room.

I tell him, "I want you to get this entire conversation. Make sure the camera angles are good, because I don't want this edited. I want this whole showdown to be on TV."

He nods. "Okay. But how late are y'all gonna be? I've got to get up early to shoot breakfast at Mystique and Zac's villa."

"This won't take long at all."

Finally a knock on the door. I take a peek to make sure it's Dreya before I swing the door open.

She comes into the room and takes notice of the four pairs of hostile eyes staring her down.

"What's wrong with y'all? What y'all looking all crazy for?" she asks.

"We went on the Internet today," I say.

Dreya bursts into laughter. "Oh, you're talking about my little interviews? Did you like them?"

"No, I didn't," I reply. "Why would you try to say my album is Disney when I'm the one who wrote all of your music?"

Dreya glances over her shoulder at the cameraman and

chuckles. "Oh, so this is how you're gonna try to get a retraction? You're really funny."

"I *did* write every song on your record though. So if mine is Disney, then what does that make yours?"

"The songs are good. The Disney part comes from your goody-goody behind," Dreya says. "Nobody wants to see that bubblegum stuff you're putting out there. All that pink and khaki you be wearing is nauseating."

"So you're straight with trying to play me to the bloggers?" I ask. "Because this is not what family does, Dreya. Family sticks together."

"You know they took that stuff out of context, Sunday, and you know I ride hard for you. Stop playing."

"I don't feel like you're riding hard for anybody but yourself," I say.

"Myself first . . . then you, boo."

Bethany's phone buzzes. And then it buzzes again. She still doesn't check her messages.

Everyone's attention goes from Dreya to Bethany. If Bethany is innocent, that scary look on her face is sure saying otherwise.

"Who in the world is blowing you up?" Dreya asks. "Sorry, Dilly, it's probably someone else's boyfriend. That's what she does."

"Don't be a hater all your life," Bethany says.

"Don't be a skank all of *your* life," Dreya replies.

Dilly says, "If it's nothing, Bethany, why don't you just read the text message out loud? Put everybody's mind at ease."

And by everybody he must mean himself, because I

think Dilly's the only one in the room who cares about who might be texting Bethany.

Bethany shakes her head. "No. I'm not doing that. If you don't trust me, why don't you just say it?"

Dilly stands up, walks away from Bethany and sits on the windowsill. "I. Don't. Trust. You. Not after I saw what went down with you and Truth."

Dreya bursts into laughter. "Oh, you don't have to worry that it's Truth! I'm just thinking that it's some other dude. Truth was only playing with her."

Bethany pulls her lips into a tight frown and swallows hard. I can tell she wants to say something, but for some reason she's restraining herself.

Finally, she says, "Mystique told me that I don't have to answer to any rumors. Y'all can think whatever you want to think. Dilly, I'm tripping on you. I really am. I thought we were past all that negativity. First of all, when me and Truth *did* hook up on the tour, we weren't even official yet. So how does that have anything to do with you trusting me?"

He shrugs. "I don't know. Just seeing it on the show was enough to make me not trust you. I don't care if we weren't official. We were officially flirting."

And Dilly definitely officially liked Bethany before she liked him. So her hooking up with Truth really wasn't playing Dilly. But it was playing Dreya. All day and all night.

"Listen, I didn't come down here to talk to skanks about the reason why they're skanky," Dreya says. "Sunday, you wanted to talk to me about the blogs. And, you're right. I was tripping about the Disney stuff. You're far from Disney."

My eyes widen. Is this an apology? Get the heck out of here.

"I mean," Dreya continues, "you're still no competition to me, but I was really mad when I did that interview. I had just found out you were getting a video shoot in the Caribbean when all of my stuff got shot in Atlanta. I was mad. I ain't gonna lie."

"So . . ."

"So I'm saying that I'm sorry! You gonna make me spell it out?" Dreya asks.

Is this some kind of alternate reality or something? "I can't believe you're saying sorry to me."

"I don't want my fans to think I'm some kind of mean girl after they read that post. I want the world to know that I love my cousin."

Suddenly, it dawns on me. Dreya is one smarty-pants heifer. This was all part of her plan! Say some crazy stuff about me online and work it into my show, so she can have the spotlight and look like everything's cool between us. That way she can smear me and still come out smelling like a rose.

And I played right into it.

The games she's playing are dirty. But I can't stoop to her level. That's not who I am and it's not what would make my mother proud.

So I chalk it. I shock the dummy out of Dreya by walking up to her and giving her a hug. She's the one looking uncomfortable.

"I love you too, Dreya. And I want you to know that there's room enough for both of us at the top. Let's both promise to not trash-talk each other in the blogs."

Dreya gives me the little half smile that she always does when she's lying. Then she says, "Of course, I promise."

Well, even if she's not being truthful . . . at least the whole BET audience can love the way she lies. . . .

21

Zac is finally on the island, so Mystique thought it would be fun if everyone got together and had breakfast. Everyone in our group, except Dreya and Truth, is here sitting outside Zac and Mystique's villa eating a catered spread.

Zac is seated at one end of the table and Big D at the other. Mystique is sitting at Zac's right. I'm sure there's some kind of pretend-rapper-mafia connection to this, but it's whatever.

I'm sitting on the other side of Mystique. I whisper to her, "Is Dreya not coming?"

"Oh, wow! I totally forgot about Dreya," Mystique says.

I don't believe that for one instant. She knew exactly what she was doing when she conveniently forgot to invite Dreya to this breakfast.

"I'm gonna go and get her," I say as I stand at the table. "We just made this pact and shared our cousinly love last night. I'm trying to keep the peace, you know."

Mystique shakes her head. "I don't know why you're going. You know she's in her room still asleep."

There is a high probability that Dreya is asleep in her room. This I don't deny. But since I was the one who told her that there was room enough at the top for us both, I have to act like I meant it, right?

"Oh, Sunday, sit down. We can send one of the butlers to get her," Mystique says.

"Now you know she's not getting up for a butler. Just let me do it. It will only take a few minutes."

I guess the BET cameraman thinks there's going to be drama when I go to Dreya's room because he gets up and follows me. It's always kind of weird when one of the cameramen is walking with me and I'm by myself. I always get the urge to turn around and talk to him, when I know I'm supposed to pretend he isn't there.

If the BET guy had a hunch there would be some drama going on, he was right! If I can judge by the ridiculous amount of noise we hear as we approach Dreya's room, it's a major ruckus. It sounds like someone's throwing something across the room.

As I lift my hand to knock on the door it swings open and Truth backs out the door. "Oh, hey, Sunday," he says. "Your cousin is crazy."

"I'm crazy, huh?" Drama hurls something through the air—a shoe—and thank God it misses the target.

I mouth the word *camera* to Dreya to try to get her to bring her anger down a notch. It doesn't work.

"I know, Sunday," she says. "I don't care if the world knows how big of a dog he is."

I step into her room, and purposely close the door behind me. Technically, the BET cameras are supposed to be able to record in every room that Epsilon Records pays for and public areas, but since Truth paid for this room (Dreya was supposed to be in one of the smaller rooms like Bethany and Regina) the cameras really can't come in here without permission.

"What did he do?" I ask.

"He's been kicking it with some girl. I caught him texting her last night in the bathroom."

"And he let you see the text? He's stupid."

Dreya shakes her head. "No, he wouldn't let me see his phone. That's what we're arguing about this morning. I asked to see his phone and he wouldn't show it to me."

"Okay, okay, calm down, though. Everyone's at breakfast and I just came to see if you wanted to eat with us."

"Oh, please, Sunday. Don't act like you care about Truth being a dog or if I even have breakfast. The cameras aren't on you now, so you can be for real. You don't really care anything about what happens to me. No one does, except maybe my mom."

I shake my head. "Why are you dead set on being in this all by yourself?"

"What do you want, Sunday?" Dreya asks. "Why are you even here?"

"We're at Zac's villa having breakfast."

"And y'all just accidentally forgot to tell me about it?"

I throw my hands into the air. "Wasn't my thing to tell you about. It was Mystique's breakfast."

"She keeps treating me foul like she's trying to destroy me or something. I'm gonna show her and everybody else."

I sit down next to my cousin. At first, I want to remind Dreya that she's not played nice with Mystique since day one. Dreya picked beef with Mystique like that strategy would catapult her into the spotlight. But Mystique's defense was always subtle and out of the public eye, which just made Dreya look like a whiny, jealous hater. Basically, Dreya made this bed.

"I don't think Mystique cares one way or the other about you, Dreya, and that's not necessarily a bad thing."

"She only hates me so much because she's afraid I'm coming to take that number-one spot. And I am."

I roll my eyes. "Okay, if we're not going to have a real conversation, Dreya, I'm going to go back to my fresh pineapple and banana bread."

"What do you mean a real conversation?"

"You're tripping," I say. "Talking about you're gonna show Mystique! Why don't you attempt to be friends with her? She is not that bad."

Dreya stands up and paces the room. "Can't you see what's happening, Sunday? They were supposed to make me a star, but then you came along and everyone is trying to play me."

"You're so busy looking at what's going on with me that you can't focus on yourself!" I say, feeling the anger rise inside me. "You need to work on your image. That drama-queen stuff is played out. I don't know how many people have to tell you that."

Dreya shakes her head. "Sunday, just go ahead to

breakfast without me. I've got to figure out what's happening with me and Truth, and I don't feel like playing nice in front of the cameras."

"Why don't we record a duet?" I ask.

"A duet?"

"Like when Brandy and Monica did 'The Boy Is Mine.' That was a big hit for them. I think we could do something similar."

Dreya looks like she considers the idea for a split second; then her eyes darken. "You're always trying to save the day, Sunday. Nah, I think I need to separate myself from this clique, and start over fresh while I still have time."

"We're family, Dreya. This ain't got nothing to do with a clique."

"It's got everything to do with it."

Dreya picks up the pillows and blankets strewn around the room. Her eyes light up when she sees what I see, a BlackBerry Torch on the floor. Truth must've dropped his cell phone in his hurry to leave the room.

She picks it up and starts pressing buttons. "Dang, it's locked. Of course it's locked. His sneaky behind wouldn't leave a phone without a code."

"Maybe that's for the best."

Dreya rolls her eyes at me. "Go ahead to your little Mystical Sounds–clique breakfast. I'm going to figure out his code, because it shouldn't be too hard."

I shake my head. "All right then, Dreya. The girls are supposed to be going out tonight to a Bajan restaurant in The Gap. You coming?"

"The girls? Is Bethany coming?"

"Yeah, I'm pretty sure she'll be there."

Dreya laughs out loud. "Sometimes, you're just plain old dingy, Sunday. Why would I want to go anywhere with her?"

"Because you're the one who said that you wanted to be wherever the cameras went. I'm just trying to help you accomplish *your* goal."

"Thanks, but no thanks. Where are the guys gonna be?"

I shrug. "Zac's taking them all somewhere."

Dreya's face twists into a frown. "Truth is not going *anywhere* without me."

"That's between y'all. I'm going back to breakfast."

It's a good thing the BET cameraman is not in this room, because the look of desperation on Dreya's face as she crumples to the floor and presses buttons on the phone, is not made for TV.

When I get back to the breakfast table, Truth is there chilling like he and Dreya didn't just have a major fall-out. I roll my eyes at him before taking my seat between Mystique and Sam.

Sam whispers to me, "Everything okay?"

I shake my head no. "They're tripping. Again. As usual."

"So," Mystique says, "I just told Big D and Zac about your video contest, Sunday."

Big D nods. "Yeah, Sunday. That was a good idea. Get the fans engaged from the jump. That's a great idea."

"I wasn't really thinking of it from a marketing perspective," I say. "I just thought it might end the argument between Mystique and Lena."

"Well, however you came up with the idea, it was a good one."

My cell phone rings, and I get up from the table to answer it.

"Do you have to get that now?" Mystique asks, sounding quite annoyed.

"Yes. It's my mom. I haven't talked to her since yesterday."

Mystique gives me a dismissive hair flip like she's annoyed I'm going to talk to my mother. She needs to stop tripping.

"Hi, Mom."

"Sunday, you haven't heard from Carlos, have you?"

I can hear the alarm in my mother's voice and it scares me too. "No, I haven't. What's wrong, Mommy?"

"I thought he would try to contact you, but I'm glad he didn't. He's in jail in Atlanta."

"What? Oh my goodness! What is he even doing in ATL? I thought you said he was in Indiana."

"He was, but apparently he's back. He and his goon cousins tried to rob Club Pyramids last night, after the club closed."

My jaw drops. "Are you serious?"

"Yep. I'm just glad you kids were nowhere near the place. There was a shootout. Bryce got shot, but I hear he's fine and already released from the hospital."

"I don't think they've told Dilly," I say as I glance back at the breakfast table. There's no way they told Dilly about the shooting, because he's still having a great time.

"Well, don't tell him, then," my mother says. "His sister will call when she wants him to know. I only called you because I thought Carlos would be crazy enough to call you from jail."

"Mom, are you okay?"

I can hear my mother's sigh over the phone. It sounds heavy, sad, and full of regret. "I am okay. I think I'm getting to a happy place again. I had been holding out the hope that Carlos had given you that money, but when I found out it was your father . . . I just didn't hold on to Carlos anymore."

I turn my back to everyone, including the camera, because I don't want them to see me tearing up. As ratchet and raggedy as Carlos was, he was the closest thing I had to a father. He and my mother had been together for three years. That's the longest she's ever dated a guy since she split up from my biological father.

Now she's back at square one. I'm sad for her and with her.

I'm here in Barbados enjoying the fab life, and my mom is back home enduring the heartbreak of a deadbeat boyfriend. Something about that doesn't seem fair.

Isn't it crazy how it can be the best of times and the worst of times at the same time?

22

"We're about to go on a tour of Harrison's Cave," I say to the cameras in my confessional. "It sounds like a lot of fun."

"Is everyone going?" the producer asks.

I know he's asking, in a roundabout way, if Dreya is going on the cave adventure with us. I haven't even asked her, to be honest, and it doesn't have anything to do with Bethany or Truth. Dreya is not a nature girl at all. She is in no way, shape, or form in touch with anything outdoors.

"Have you met Dreya?" I ask. Immediately I regret this sound bite, because I know they can use this whenever they please, and completely out of context.

"Everyone is not going," I continue. "Dreya doesn't do caves, and Dilly is still under the weather. The only ones going are me, Sam, Mystique, and Zac."

The producer motions to the cameraman to stop shooting. I guess I'm too boring for him this afternoon. Whatever.

I leave the hotel room and meet up with Sam, Mystique, and Zac outside of Zac's villa. I laugh out loud when I see Mystique's shoes. They are some kind of designer, ten-inch, heels.

"What are you tripping on?" Sam asks.

I point at the shoes. "Mystique, you do know we're going to a *cave* right?"

"Yes." She looks down at her feet. "What's wrong with my shoes? They have a tram and an elevator."

"But once you get inside the cave, you have to walk on some pretty uneven surfaces," I reply.

"Well, I'll just skip that part."

Zac says, "Babe, maybe you want to put on some sneakers. The best part of the cave is the walking part. You won't be able to see anything good with those heels on."

Mystique sighs and motions for me to follow her back into the villa. She goes straight to one of her gigantic trunks and pulls out two pairs of sneakers.

"Which pair?" she asks.

"Either, I guess. They both match."

Mystique shakes her head and says, "How can they both match? One is white and the other is black. One has to be better than the other."

"It's not like this is a red-carpet affair. We're going to a cave."

"You've never had your fashion choices ripped apart by a blogger, so you don't understand. Once, I was on my way to Target, and I was wearing a cute jogging suit with my favorite workout sneakers. They called my look 'hobo chic.' "

I cover my mouth to hold in my giggle. "How do you know that wasn't a compliment?"

"It was Sandra Rose."

I can't help it now, the giggles just tumble out. "Sandra Rose is funny. You shouldn't take that stuff so seriously. I think some of the bloggers post that kind of stuff just so people will click on their page, and they can get advertising money."

"It was mean," Mystique says. "And now, I can't go out without wondering what she's going to put in her blog about me."

"So why don't you do your own blog? Get the bloggers back?" I ask.

"Because it's so much easier to pretend to rise above it. You can't win a fight with someone who throws rocks and then hides behind their laptop."

I point at the black shoes. "Those match the best."

She's wearing black shorts and a silver baby tee. She looks glamorous in everything she puts on, which is why I'm totally surprised that she cares what the bloggers have to say. She could wear a plastic bag and flip-flops and still look hot.

"Come on, girl, before Zac starts fussing about me taking too long."

As we hurry back to the guys, I think about how normal Zac and Mystique are in their relationship. I mean they are both multi-platinum multimillionaires and they have the most regular conversations and disagreements.

I wonder if Sam and I will have the same kind of relationship.

But Sam and I are kind of lopsided, or unevenly yoked as my mother would call it. I'm blowing up and he's still on the come up.

When we get back to the guys, there is a car waiting for us. A normal car. Not a limo or some kind of luxury sedan. This is out of the ordinary for Zac and Mystique. They always travel in excessive luxury. The BET cameraman is going to have to follow in another car, because there's barely enough room in this little hatchback for the four of us.

"What's going on with Truth and Drama?" Mystique asks as we squeeze into the backseat. Zac sits in the front, and I'm sandwiched between Mystique and Sam.

"I don't know. Their typical stuff, I guess. She's jealous beyond reason and he just does stuff to make her even more jealous."

"Enough about those two," Zac says. "I've got some better news."

"What is it?" Mystique asks.

"It's not for you babe, it's for Sam."

Sam perks up and cheeses. "What's popping?"

"Well, I've been listening to the music you and Sunday put together for Bethany and Drama, and the tracks you did for Truth's album. You are too talented to be wasting away in Big D's basement."

Sam swallows hard. "What do you mean?"

"I mean you should be working for me, for my label. With a real budget, real equipment, and real perks. You shouldn't be a roadie on tour, man. You're a producer."

Sam says, "Big D has been good to me, don't get it twisted."

"See, Mystique. That's what I'm talking about," Zac says. "Loyalty. People are loyal to you when you treat them well. It's a lesson Drama should learn."

I hear what Zac is saying, but I can't believe my ears. Is he actually offering Sam a job and is Sam turning it down to stay with Big D?

"But anyway," Zac says, "I'm not saying anything bad about Big D. He's given you a start in the industry. He's groomed you for bigger and better things. He would think you were crazy to turn down this opportunity."

"What exactly is the opportunity?" Sam asks. "You haven't actually said it yet."

"I want you to come work for me at my New York office. You'd split time between NYC and ATL, but the bulk of my new talent is in New York."

Hold up and wait a minute! Sam and I are just now getting the boyfriend/girlfriend swag on lock, and here comes Zac messing up our flow.

"I gave Zac some of Sam's tracks," Mystique says. "And he is completely blown away."

"Sam is supposed to be going to Georgia Tech in the fall," I say.

Sam gives me a look that I can't decipher. It's not angry, but maybe it's hurt. Yeah, that's it. He looks like I just pinched him or something.

"School can wait if I'm going to get a chance to work on some multimillion-dollar projects," Sam says. "But I need to talk to Big D and see how he feels about it. He's never steered me wrong before."

"That's fair enough, and I like that you respect that relationship enough to not burn any bridges. You're smart, Sam, and I think you'll go far in the industry with that attitude."

Who cares how far he goes in the industry? If he's in New York City, how in the world is he supposed to be my college boyfriend?

I don't say anything else for the remainder of the thirty-minute drive to Harrison's Cave. The drive is scenic enough that I can just pretend to be taking in the sights. But really, I'm in trip-out mode and I'm torn. I want Sam to get his big break, don't get me wrong. I just don't want it to take him away from me.

When we get to the cave, the first thing we do is sit for a while in the Visitor Reception Center. There is a cruise ship coming in and they don't want to start the tour without them.

As we're sitting on a bench in the middle of the room, Mystique says, "Could we be any more on display than this? I'm not feeling this, Zac. And we're taking the tour with a whole cruise ship full of people?"

"It could be a bunch of old people who don't even recognize you," I say.

Zac says, "Or it could be your fans, which would be even better. Imagine how much a fan would love to say they went on a tour of Harrison's Cave with Mystique."

When this doesn't seem to appease Mystique, Zac says, "Okay, I'll see if we can go ahead and start the tour."

"Thank you, baby."

Mystique frowns and folds her arms across her chest. I think she's just mad that the staff at the cave didn't do anything special or roll out the red carpet for her. Mystique arrived on the scene and it was just business as usual.

Actually, now that I think about it, it's kind of funny!

What's not funny is the scowl on Sam's face. I know he means it for me too, because he keeps tossing it over in my direction. I also know it has something to do with his offer from Zac, but I'm not about to ask him. Not while he's looking like that, and not when an argument is looming over our new romance like a storm cloud.

Zac walks back up with one of the cave employees. It looks like a manager.

"Ms. Mystique, please accept our apologies. The workers simply did not recognize you, but we would love to allow you and your party access to the cave in a private viewing."

Mystique's frown melts away and she becomes that syrupy sweet, loving, and humble pop star again.

"It's really not a problem," she says. "We wouldn't want to trouble you at all. Is it too much trouble?"

"No! Not at all. I would love to be your own personal tour guide. We love your music in Barbados."

Mystique smiles as she stands to her feet. I almost burst into laughter when she gives the manager a little handshake and hug like she's the Queen of England. I can tell Sam is trying not to laugh too. Zac grins and rolls his eyes as the clearly enamored manager locks arms with Mystique and leads her to the glass elevator that descends to the caves.

I jab Sam in the ribs as we follow the group. "What's up, Sam? Why you looking all twisted?"

He shrugs, but doesn't reply. Hmmm . . . it's worse than I thought.

As we ride down from the cliff to the bottom of the valley, we listen to the chirpy manager give much history about the cave. Typically, I like listening to this type of scientific stuff, but I can't do anything but focus on Sam's deepened frown.

After the elevator ride, we're led to a tram that looks like a miniature version of one of the roller-coaster rides at Six Flags.

I slide in next to Sam, and he folds his arms against his chest and tightens his lips.

I ask, "Are you going to keep looking crazy, or are you going to tell me what's on your mind? I'm not a mind reader, you know."

Sam ignores me and locks his seat belt. I cannot believe he's just ignoring my questions like I haven't said anything.

The tram ride is forty minutes long, and Sam sits here and gives me the silent treatment for the entire forty minutes. Finally, it's over and we're in the heart of the cave, underground, with beauty all around us. We get out of the tram so that we can explore.

Sam tries to march away from me, but I meet him step for step. I follow him to a far corner of the cave where the stalactites jut out from the ceiling like limestone icicles. For a moment, I'm so caught up in the beauty of the cave that I forget about Sam's foul mood.

"Isn't this beautiful?" I ask. "I've never seen anything like this in my life."

He spins around and says, "Sunday, I'm angry because

you weren't happy for me when Zac offered me the job. There. Now leave me alone so I can get my head right. Go explore the cave with Mystique."

"No. Not before I say that you're right."

"Huh?"

"I wasn't happy when I first heard it, because all I could think about was us being separated."

Sam's nose flares. "I would've been happy for you, Sunday. I've been happy for you with every new thing that's come your way."

I take one of Sam's hands in mine, and I feel him relax. "I know, I know. I am glad for you now, though, and I think Big D will be too."

"I don't know about Big D, Sunday. I really need you to have my back, because I don't think he's gonna want to lose me. He doesn't have another producer and Epsilon is snatching up his best artists."

"So he can just do what he does best, right? Develop new talent."

"But Big D has always wanted to blow up too. I wish Epsilon Records would give him some kind of honorary executive gig with a big office and a window."

"You think that maybe we can make that happen?" I ask. "I mean, Big D is my manager. He's always gonna be in my camp. He's got my back, and I trust him."

Sam shakes his head. "We don't have the pull yet to make that happen, but maybe one day."

"Until then, he's not going to hold you back from you doing what you gotta do, Sam. Big D's heart is too big for all that."

"What about you, Sunday? You're not going to have a change of heart about me, are you?"

"You mean about you working for Zac, or our relationship?"

"Both. Are you gonna be okay if I blow up too? Are you still gonna be my boo?"

I give Sam a gigantic smile. "You're gonna be my boo whether you blow up or not. You just better remember that when those NYC groupie chicks push up on you."

Sam chuckles quietly as if a big laugh might disturb the cave.

"I don't know what you're laughing about. I hear the New York groupies are on a whole other level than the ones in ATL."

"Well, I wouldn't know, and I don't want to know . . . because I only want one girl."

"That would be me?" I ask sweetly.

Sam kisses my forehead. "That would be you."

23

We're back at the hotel, getting ready for our night in St. Lawrence Gap or De Gap if you're one of the Bajan locals. Bethany tries on outfits and models them for me and Dilly (who looks a hundred-percent better).

I can't keep my mind off of Sam, though. He took a walk with Big D to tell him about Zac's offer. I think Big D saw it coming, because the look on his face was of quiet resignation. I think he knows that we can all be bigger than Atlanta local artists, but I just hope he doesn't feel slighted by Sam's departure from Big D in the A Records.

"What about this one?" Bethany asks.

It's a clingy silver tube dress that she's coupled with some black and silver heeled sandals. It looks very good on her and it hugs every one of her ample curves. I think it's hot, but Dilly frowns.

"You're not wearing that," Dilly says.

"Why not?"

"Because I don't want any guys trying to look at my girl."

Bethany looks at me and we both crack up laughing.

"Dilly, you aren't her daddy," I say. "Nor are you her husband. Stop tripping! Boyfriends don't get to tell their girlfriends what to do."

"Okay, okay," Dilly says, hands raised in defeat. "I'm asking you not to wear that. I'm asking if you would please, please wear something that covers a little bit more of your body."

Bethany pokes her lips out and puts a hand on her hip. "What if I say no?"

"Then I'm going to be forced to not hang with the guys all night and follow you all over The Gap."

Bethany laughs out loud. "Okay, I'll change, but not because you told me to, but because I want you to have fun and not be miserable."

"Thank you," Dilly says with a satisfied grin.

Bethany goes into the bedroom to change into something else. While she's out of the sitting room, her cell phone buzzes on the table. Then it buzzes again.

Dilly and I make eye contact.

His chest heaves up and down. I know he's trying to keep himself from grabbing that phone. I see his restraint slipping. . . .

"Don't . . ." I say.

But it's too late. Dilly picks up the BlackBerry and reads the text messages. It must be all bad because he bites his lip, swallows hard, and drops the phone on the floor.

"I-I gotta go," he says before making a mad dash to the door.

Crap! Crap! Crap!

Bethany comes back out of the bedroom wearing a cute jean-short onesie, and a scarf around her neck.

"Where's Dilly?" she asks.

I just shake my head and point to her BlackBerry.

She gulps.

Crap! Crap! Crap!

"I can explain," Bethany says as she retrieves her BlackBerry.

I shake my head. "Don't explain anything to me. Explain it to your boyfriend."

She reads the text messages and groans. Then she growls. "I hate Truth. I really, really hate him."

"You still messing with him?" I ask.

"No, I'm not still messing with him, but he won't leave me alone. He's been texting me since we've been down here trying to get me to meet up with him."

"And you told him no."

"Of course I told him no! Why do you sound so suspicious?"

Is she seriously asking me this question? She's the one who steals everybody's boyfriends and does everyone dirty. How can she expect me *not* to sound suspicious of her?

"Bethany, you're tripping. Dilly is a good guy, and he really likes you. You should've been up-front with him. How do you expect him to believe anything you say to him now?"

"I can show him all my sent messages where I told Truth to stop texting me."

I bite my lip and think on this a moment. I don't know if it'll be enough to make Dilly believe her. She's got too much of a history of being foul. But even though she's got history, the tears in her eyes make me think that she might be telling the truth.

Finally, I say, "My mother always tells me that you don't ever have to prove you're telling the truth because God always reveals a lie."

"But there's no lie here, only a misunderstanding."

"I guess you have to try to make him understand. But do it quickly. Don't give him too much time to think about it."

"Where were the guys meeting before they leave?"

"At Zac's villa."

"Will you go with me? I can't have Dilly thinking this about me all night long. I just can't."

Bethany is full-on crying now and as much as I hate to admit it, I truly believe her. I've seen her tell lies, so I could basically be a human lie detector when it comes to Bethany. I just hope that Dilly believes her too, else the BET cameras are going to have some drama-filled breakup footage to add to their collection.

24

"Is Dilly here?" Bethany asks Mystique when we get to Zac's villa.

Mystique has got her party clothes on—a bright colorful mini dress and yellow heels. She flips her wig out of her face and appraises Bethany. She looks her up and down and then takes her tear-streaked face into her hand.

"What's wrong with you?" she asks. "And does it have anything to do with why you're looking for Dilly?"

Bethany glances at the BET cameraman out the corner of her eye. "I-I just need to talk to him."

"I don't want any drama tonight!" Mystique says. "Y'all youngsters stay mad and arguing about something. We're in Barbados, for crying out loud! Let your hair down and have some fun. Y'all too dang intense all the time."

I clear my throat. "Um, that . . . well, that was pretty

intense, Mystique. Maybe you should go lie down and chill for a minute."

She looks at me and smiles. "Okay, Captain Obvious, you got me. That was kind of intense, but y'all are getting on my nerves with all this teen angst."

"We're teenagers," I say. "What do you expect?"

Bethany gives a big sigh. "I just love how y'all are making jokes when I've got a serious issue to attend to. Is Dilly here or not?"

"He's not here. Try him and Sam's room."

Bethany turns to leave, but I hold up one hand. I dial Sam's cell phone number.

"Hey, boo," he says with a chuckle.

I want to stay serious for Bethany's face, but I can't stop the smile from exploding onto my face. "Hey, boo! Is Dilly there with you?"

"Naw. I thought he was in y'all room."

"He ran out."

"Good grief. Why did he run out? What happened?"

"Tell you lata. Amera-cay."

Sam says, "The camera dude is near you?"

"Yeppers."

"Okay, so just answer my questions with yes or no responses."

"Okay."

"Is Bethany playing Dilly again?"

"No . . . I don't think so."

"Does Dilly think she's playing him again?"

"Yes."

"Does Dilly think she's playing him with Truth?"

"Yes."

Sam says, "I'm sick of their triangle. Bethany ain't all that for these dudes to be getting so twisted over."

"You just got extra points by saying that, you know."

Sam laughs. "I didn't know we were taking score."

"I'm *always* taking score. Right now you're ahead. Keep that in mind while you're out with Zac tonight."

Bethany taps my shoulder. Hard. Okay, I know girlfriend is stressed, but she needs to fall back with the physical contact. I look down at her finger like it's a bug I'm going to squash and she quickly removes it.

"Is he there?" she asks.

Oh, duh. This is the reason I called in the first place.

"No, Sam thought he was still with us."

"I'll tell Dilly to call you if I see him," Sam says.

"Okay. Bye."

I disconnect the phone and turn to Bethany. "Looks like you're just going to have to wait until Dilly wants to be found."

Bethany's tears start up again. "I can't go out with him thinking . . . what he thinks about me."

It's funny how we're speaking in code around the cameras now. Nobody, no matter how much money you're paying them, wants all of their business on a TV show for the world to see.

"So don't go out with us, then. Sit in your hotel room, crying your eyes out, while Sunday and I enjoy some reggae music and good food."

Bethany rolls her eyes at Mystique. "I don't see how you can be so mean, Mystique. I'm going to find Dilly."

She storms out of the villa and Mystique shrugs. "Like I said, teen drama. That's why I like you, Sunday. You're so much more mature than your cronies."

I don't know if I'm so much more mature than everybody else, I just don't like people in my business. And the BET cameras are putting the entire country in Dilly and Bethany's mix as soon as this thing airs. I thought this show was gonna be about my video shoot, but there's a lot more happening than that.

Zac comes out of the bedroom and looks Mystique up and down, from head to toe and back up to her head. "We should've brought your bodyguard, Mystique. I don't know how I feel about you going to the club unprotected, and dressed like that."

"Are you kidding me, Zac? They don't even know who I am in this country. I only get recognized in the resort, and that's because there's more Americans here than anywhere on the island."

"Just because the people at the cave didn't know you, that doesn't mean that someone else won't. Why don't y'all just hang with us?"

Mystique frowns. "But we were having a ladies' night out."

"I know, but I would feel more *comfortable* if you went with us."

My eyes dart back and forth between Mystique and Zac. This is clearly a battle of wills. Mystique lifts an eyebrow and smirks.

"All right. We'll. Go. With. You."

Uh-oh. Although we're going with the guys now, I

have an idea who actually won this battle. I don't think it's over, but it won't be played out on TV either.

I'm so glad to hear the knock on the villa door, because the moment of tension between Mystique and Zac is too much for me. It's like watching your parents fight. Like what kid wants to see their parents argue?

But when Zac opens the door to Dreya and Truth, my big sigh lets everyone know what I'm thinking. Wish I could just have a fun evening!

Dreya is wearing heavy makeup, eye shadow, mascara, and eyeliner, but I can still tell that her eyes are puffy, swollen, and red. She's been crying her eyes out, probably all day. Her entire face is swollen, really, probably also the effect of her tears.

I guess she figured out the password on Truth's phone.

But Truth is looking real relaxed like there's nothing wrong. I know my cousin. *Something* is wrong. Maybe she hasn't mentioned it to him yet.

"Where are we going?" Dreya asks.

"A reggae club in The Gap," Zac says. "Soon as Sam gets here, we're out."

"Isn't Big D coming?" I ask.

Zac shakes his head. "Nah. He's staying here with his lady. I invited him, but he declined my invitation."

Hmmm . . . what's that about? *He declined my invitation.* Zac sounds like he might be offended by Big D turning him down. But for real, if I was Big D, I wouldn't be trying to grin and cheese all up in Zac's face pretending to be friends. Zac is taking Big D's main producer, if Sam says yes, and that's not really a friend move.

Finally Sam shows up. He looks good in standard Sam apparel—black tee, jeans, black sneakers. Chain on his neck, cap on his head. Typical, low-key Sam. Hotness.

"What took you so long?" I ask.

"I like to keep the ladies waiting," Sam says.

After everyone cracks up laughing, Sam says, "Wow. But seriously, I went to talk to Big D."

"And?" Zac asks.

"It's all good," Sam replies. "We'll talk business tomorrow. But tonight I'm ready to chill."

Zac slightly narrows his eyes as if he doesn't like Sam's response. I don't think Zac is used to being kept waiting by anyone. Especially a new producer to whom he's just offered the deal of a lifetime. But I appreciate Sam and his swagger. A dude with swagger never lets the next man see him sweat.

"Well, if we're all here, let's go! I'm hungry for some jerk chicken," Mystique says. She's regained her cool diva-like composure, but I'm sure that Zac is gonna get it later when the cameras are no longer rolling.

We all ride in a limo van like the one that brought us to the resort from the airport. Dreya is uncharacteristically silent, and the smile she has plastered on her face is fake as all get-out. The first opportunity I get, I'm pulling her to the side to get the scoop.

When the limo driver pulls off, Mystique says, "It's a good thing Bethany and Dilly didn't go with us, since Truth and Drama decided to roll. That would've been awkward."

Now see, this is Mystique trying to start something in

front of the camera. I stare at Dreya, trying to send her mental signals. . . . *Don't take the bait!*

"Why would that have been awkward?" Dreya asks.

Clearly, my cousin missed the signal. We've got to work on our telepathy. When we were little, we used to be like the wonder-twin cousins or something.

Mystique says, "You know, with what happened on the tour and all."

"Oh!" Dreya says with a phony chuckle. "You mean the fact that Bethany is a slut and was hooking up with my man?"

Oh no . . . the carefully placed façade is cracking. Dreya's about to let loose. And Mystique is poking the bear.

"Yeah, but I guess y'all hashed that all out because you and Truth are still together. Like it couldn't be me. If Zac did that . . ."

Zac says, "Why you gotta put me in that discussion? This is about Truth and Drama."

"I'm just saying," Mystique says.

I'm not liking this side of Mystique. This catty, disliking-Dreya side of Mystique. I know that Dreya has said some twisted stuff about Mystique, but I feel caught in the middle of that. I'd feel like dirt choosing Mystique over my cousin, but if they keep this up, it's going to come down to a choice.

"Maybe Dreya was just able to forgive him. There's nothing wrong with forgiving someone," I say.

Truth gives me a fist bump across the seat with the hand that's not wrapped around Dreya and holding her close. Dreya looks like a ticking time bomb.

"I forgive, but I don't forget, and I'm not stupid," Dreya says.

Are we there yet? Because all of a sudden it's starting to feel cramped in this ginormous limo.

"No one said you were stupid, baby," Truth says. He plants a kiss on her cheek.

Dreya untangles herself from Truth's arm and sits straight up. "Yeah, you think I'm stupid. You *and* Bethany think I'm stupid."

Big sigh. Here we go.

"Wh-what do you mean, babe? I'm not fooling with no Bethany."

Dreya leans right in Truth's face. Nose to nose. "That's only because she told your raggedy, busted-up self, that she didn't want you."

Truth looks surprised and furious as he wipes Dreya's spittle off the bridge of his nose. "I *said* I don't know what you mean."

Dreya laughs out loud. "I'm not stupid, *babe*, but you are. If you're gonna be sending reckless texts to someone else's girlfriend, don't you think you should put a better password on your phone than your birthday, you big dummy!"

"I told you to stop going through my phone," Truth says.

"I told *you* to stop cheating on me, but clearly neither of us has been listening very well," Dreya replies.

"Hey, why don't y'all chill?" Zac says. "We're all trying to have a good time here."

"You ain't my daddy," Dreya says. "I know everybody's treating you like you're some kind of don or something. You need to fall back and mind your business."

"Don't you talk to my man like that," Mystique says.

Dreya just laughs in her face. "You do *not* want it with me."

Truth says, "Drama, why don't we just talk this out when we get to the club. Ain't no need to bring Mystique and Zac into this. They don't have anything to do with this."

Sam and I are silent. I'm not saying anything because I'll be darned if I take a side this time. Plus, I'm waiting to see if Truth thinks he's gonna manhandle my cousin. Because it's not going down like that tonight.

"You don't tell me what to do either, Truth. You need to start explaining, right now, why you were sending Bethany text messages."

Truth chuckles. "All right, since you want to try and put me on blast in front of everybody, Bethany still wants me. She hasn't stopped wanting me since day one. And if you keep tripping, I'm gonna give her what she wants."

"Obviously she DON'T want you because she sent you about five texts that said, 'NO THANKS, I'm with Dilly.'"

"She's just playing hard to get," Truth says.

Sam shakes his head. "Dude, you can't be serious."

"All these chicks want me—Sunday too if you want to get down to it," Truth says.

Before I can reply, Dreya says, "Nobody wants you. Least of all me. Sunday, can I stay in your room for the rest of the weekend?"

"Of course."

Then, Truth just loses it! In a lightning-fast move he wraps his hand around Dreya's throat and snatches her head back against the seat.

"Truth, get off of her!" I yell. "Stop the camera! Stop filming THIS!"

Sam knocks the camera out of the cameraman's hand before he can acquiesce. When he reaches down to pick it up, Zac shakes his head, no. The cameraman sits back in his seat. I guess he knows better than to cross Zillionaire.

Slowly, Truth removes his hand from Dreya's neck and she coughs violently. As Truth leans back and relaxes, as if he's proved something, Zac jumps across the seat and puts Truth in a headlock. Truth struggles to free himself with no success.

Zac says, "I guess somebody told you it was okay to beat on women. Maybe it was your daddy, I don't know. But you are NOT about to manhandle this girl in my presence. You are disrespecting every woman in this car, and NOBODY disrespects my girl. So, I'ma let you take a nap right now. You fixing to go to sleep, and when you wake up you're gonna be in a cab taking your fake thug self to the airport. If you're still here tomorrow, you might need a wheelchair to get back to the States."

After a little more fruitless struggling, Truth loses consciousness. Zac then turns to the BET cameraman. "That better not show up on TV, or you're gonna lose more than your job, son."

Son? The cameraman has to be twice Zac's age. He's tripping on some old straight gangsta type stuff.

But, I am glad he handled Truth. I just don't know

what the aftermath of this will be for Dreya, Big D, or Truth's record deal with Epsilon Records.

All this over Bethany? I never understand guys who would put everything on the line for a whole bunch of nothing! Truth's gonna wake up in the morning feeling really, really dumb about all this. Really, really, dumb.

"Zac, baby, did you really have to do that?" Mystique asks.

"Yeah, I did," he replies softly.

Dreya bursts into tears. No one moves to offer her any sympathy. It's not that I feel good about Truth hurting her, it's that she is *always* ruining something for me! This reality show, this trip, this music thing! I wish Dreya and all of her drama would just disappear out of my life.

And she can take her raggedy woman-beating boyfriend with her.

25

The fight with Truth in the limo has put a damper on everyone's evening. No one is in a good mood, but we decided to still go to the reggae club anyway. One, because we're hungry and two, if we all go back to the resort, more violence is sure to erupt. Truth needs time to clear out, and we need time away from him.

For some reason, witnessing the attack has caused Mystique to go sweet on Dreya. She's been holding her hand since before we got out of the limo. Frankly, Dreya looks kind of uncomfortable with the overt showing of affection. Dreya's not the affectionate type, at all, but she still doesn't release Mystique's hand until we get into the restaurant and sit down.

"Are you all right, Dreya?" I ask as we all look at the menus. "Do you want to call Aunt Charlie?"

"No. Don't call her," Dreya says. "She's gonna trip that he's even here in the first place."

"Okay, but do you want me to call Big D to make sure he's gone when we get back to the resort?"

Zac says, "No need. I already took care of that. You don't have to worry about him anymore this weekend."

"I-I could feel his hands pressing into my throat. I couldn't breathe. Was he trying to kill me?"

Sam says, "No. He knows that no one would've let him get that off. He was just trying to scare you."

"But those few seconds hurt so bad. Was I wrong to call him out about Bethany?" Dreya's voice sounds so small and frightened. I've never seen her so shaken. But I guess seeing your life flash before your eyes, even if it is briefly, is pretty scary.

"I don't think you were wrong to call him out about Bethany, but maybe you shouldn't have done it in front of all of us. That was kind of rough," I say.

Mystique says, "That doesn't give him a reason to choke her, though."

"Definitely not excusing him," I say. "I'm just being honest."

Dreya says, "Sunday is right. I wanted to embarrass him on camera. That's why I did it, plus I was mad that he would play me like that—again. I mean seriously, is Bethany all that?"

"He's just a dog," Mystique says. "And dogs don't deserve girls like us. They deserve hoodrat, busted-up chicks."

"Not even a hoodrat deserves getting choked," Sam says. "Although a hoodrat probably would've put in some work on him as soon as he took his hands away."

A live band is playing in the tiny but lively club. I sway

back and forth to the festive drumbeat. The dance floor is packed with locals and vacationers. I can tell the difference because the resort people look a bit out of place. Their dancing is a little off the beat—shoot, a lot of them look like this is their first time dancing.

Even with everything that has gone on tonight, now I feel like dancing. Maybe it'll relieve some stress, and since the BET cameraman was so mad at Zac that he went back to the hotel, I don't have to worry about my club dancing being on TV.

"Order me some jerk chicken," I tell Mystique. "Come on, Sam, I want to dance."

Sam's eyebrows lift. "You want me to go out there?"

"Yes! It'll be fun."

"For who? You or the people who will be laughing at me when I attempt to dance?"

I give Sam a tiny smile. "You can save a girl's life, but you can't dance to an itty-bitty reggae song?"

"Aw, crap," Sam says. "Come on. It sounds like you're calling my manhood into question."

Zac laughs out loud. "Dude, she IS. And she's making you dance. You must be sprung."

When Sam doesn't reply, I say, "Well . . . are you?"

"Am I what?"

"Sprung?"

Sam laughs out loud. "I'll answer that if and when I make it off this dance floor in one piece."

"Good answer, bro!" Zac high-fives Sam as we walk away from the table.

On the way to the dance floor, I turn and ask Sam, "What did Big D say about the job offer?"

"He seemed happy for me, but he just kept cracking his knuckles."

"He does that when he's mad."

"I know. So, I asked him if he wanted me to turn the job down." Sam maneuvers us through the tight maze of tables and onto the floor.

"You did? What did he say?" Now, I'm yelling because the music is so loud.

"He totally freaked me out and started crying!"

My mouth drops open. "Get outta here! Boo-hoo crying?"

"Naw. Tears just started coming down his face. It was weird, but he said not to turn the job down."

"Big D is an emotional cat, for real," I say. I remember when he gave me a similar speech about it being destiny that we met and all that. Big D is a big ol' softie.

"I know, but I'm glad I talked to him about it, because I'm taking the offer."

The thought of Sam all the way in New York City while I'm studying in Atlanta makes me a little sad, and just a tad bit stressed, so I let the music transport me to another place. I move in time to the drumbeat, and imitate the hip motions of the other dancers. Sam does a version of what the men are doing, which ends up looking like a little jump with his hands up.

Then the fast drumbeat slows down and couples start moving in close. Sam pulls me into a very modest embrace. He knows what it is. We might be a couple, but I don't do the whole dirty-dancing thing. That's not me.

"So, when you go to college in ATL, are you going to get a replacement boyfriend since I won't be there?"

"We'll have to see. I'll have to do something to pass the time, right?"

"Sunday . . ."

I shake my head and smile. "Nope. You don't get to make the rules. You're chasing the paper, right?"

"Well, that's because I'm done chasing you. I've already caught you."

This tickles me for some reason and it makes me laugh. "Okay, dude. I'm caught . . . for now. But let me hear one story about you and some New York groupie . . ."

"You won't. I promise, you won't."

26

After a few hours at the reggae club we come back to the resort to turn in early. When Dreya and I get to my room, it suddenly dawns on me that Bethany is probably in here. Even though, this time, Bethany isn't in the wrong, Dreya probably doesn't want to deal with her tonight.

Before I open the door, I turn to Dreya. "Is there anything you need from your other room?"

"No . . . it should all be in your room. Zac said that Shelly was going to go in and pack it up for me."

Darn. I was trying to stall for time.

"What is it? Do you not want to share with me, because I can go with Regina and Bethany if you want the room to yourself."

"So you would be cool sharing a room with Bethany?"

Dreya laughs. "Of course not, but since these rooms

are four hundred dollars a night, I'm sure not trying to spend my money."

"Oh, well then cool. Come on in. I think Bethany might be in here, so I just wanted to make sure you were okay with that."

Sure enough, Bethany is sprawled on the couch in my sitting room. She's still fully dressed, so I pull the blanket from her feet to wake her up.

She squints her eyes into tiny slits. "Sunday, is that you?"

"Yeah, girl. We're back from the club. You okay? You still have your clothes on."

She nods. "I'm cool. I found Dilly, and he doesn't believe me."

"Don't worry about that. Sam will talk to him tonight. It'll be okay in the morning."

Bethany sits up on the couch. "Are you sure? Because I really like Dilly. I think I might even love him."

I can't imagine anyone being in love with Dilly. Even though he's nice and very cute, he's ridiculously young and goofy. But to each her own, I guess.

Dreya rolls her eyes at Bethany and goes into the bedroom. Bethany watches nervously as Dreya walks by. I don't think she wants to tangle with Dreya tonight, but luckily for Bethany, Dreya doesn't have a tangling bone left in her body. Not after her run-in with Truth.

There's a knock on my room door. It's Dilly and he's standing there, redder than a Macintosh apple in a bobbing barrel. His chest is heaving up and down and he looks ready to blow up.

"What's wrong, Dilly?"

"My brother's been shot. My sister just called me."

My eyes widen in feigned surprise. "Is he okay?"

"Yes, the bullet just grazed his shoulder. He's at home."

I nod. "That's good. How are you? Are you cool?"

He pushes past me and up to Bethany. "Sam told me you weren't lying."

"I told you."

"But the fact that I didn't believe you . . . well, it makes me think that I don't trust you. And maybe I shouldn't be with a girl I can't trust."

Bethany looks down at her folded hands resting in her lap. This is a reaping-and-sowing kind of moment if you ask me. All the mess that Bethany has done. Hooking up with other people's boyfriends, playing people behind their back . . . it was kind of inevitable that it was going to come back to bite her one day.

I just didn't think it would be tonight, in my hotel room, in Barbados! I mean, come on . . . can I please just enjoy paradise?

Bethany says, "You're probably right. I don't deserve a nice guy like you anyway. Just go, if you're going to keep saying mean stuff to me. I can't take it."

"But," Dilly says, "I really like you, Bethany. You're funny, you can sing, you're pretty, and your body is bangin'."

"So are you saying we're still together?"

Dilly nods. "If you want to be."

Bethany dang near knocks me over jumping up to hug Dilly. Is it just me or was Dilly's whole speech kind of . . . well . . . twelfth grade? I mean, I know he's about to be a senior in high school, but I wish a boy would tell me "your body is bangin'" as a reason for us to get back together. Seriously?

But like I said, to each her own. I just wish they would move their party outside of my sitting room. I've got two more days in Barbados, and I plan to enjoy them so I need my beauty rest! Ya dig?

27

Lena, the video director, has got the raw footage of the video, and she wants me to watch it in Zac's villa. I invited the entire crew to come along so that they can tell me what they like the best, and give the BET camera guy some fun and positive stuff to tape. We're all wearing swim apparel, because as soon as we get done here, we're hitting the beach.

Sam and I are gonna pass on the kayaking today, though.

"So both versions of the video came out great," Lena says as we all grab a seat on either the couch or floor. "I think Epsilon will love the idea of letting the fans pick the video that will run on BET. That was a great idea."

"Yes, Sunday," Mystique says, "I agree. I called Mr. Toyomi at Epsilon and he was very excited about the idea."

Mr. Toyomi is one of the owners of Epsilon Records.

The man is a billionaire. And the fact that Mystique has his number in her cell phone ought to tell Dreya who the big fish is in this little pond. And it isn't a newbie pop upstart named Drama.

Lena says, "I'm going to play the DVD, which has the two videos back to back, and then we'll discuss."

Lena presses Play on her portable DVD player device, and the video begins.

I'm always surprised to see how I look when I'm on TV. I seem shorter than I actually am, but at least I'm still cute. Also, it's a good thing my lips are moving in time to the music. The whole lip-synching thing is harder than it looks.

Then we get to the end of the first video, and Sam kisses me. Seeing it on the screen and remembering it happen at the same time totally takes my breath away. Sam's got his chest stuck out and is grinning hard, like he is the *man* up in here. Dilly giving him a fist bump doesn't help things either.

The second video is a lot like the first one, but there are just different shots of me. It's like Lena got the opportunity to use every shot she took. There is one shot I really like of me in the second video where I'm in the sand at the edge of the Caribbean Sea with my head back. It's hotness indeed.

When we're done looking at both videos, Lena turns off the TV with a remote control.

"Mystique, what do you think? Which do you choose?" Lena asks.

Mystique twists her lips to one side and says, "It doesn't

really matter since we're going to play both of them on BET, but if I have my choice it would be the first one, even if Sam did ruin it with his vacuum lips."

Sam touches his lips self-consciously and everyone bursts into laughter.

"Hey! I'm sensitive about the soup coolers," Sam says. "Don't be calling my lips *vacuum* lips, Mystique."

"Sorry," she says. "But that's all I could think about when I saw that."

"She's a hater, Sam!" I say. "She barely has lips! That's why she's got all that lip gloss on!"

This makes everyone laugh even harder, even Mystique and Zac.

"I can't stand you insufferable teenagers!" Mystique says.

Dilly says, "You say that like you're old. You're like five years older than us."

"That's light years older in industry years," Bethany says. "She's like forty in the industry."

Mystique's mouth drops open. "Um, no, ma'am. I'm not forty, no matter who's doing the counting."

Dreya sits quietly while we clown about the video. I don't know if she doesn't have anything to say, or if she doesn't want to participate in all the fun when she's feeling so sad. There are bruises forming on her neck, where Truth choked her, and she's not even attempting to cover them up. She's acting like her wounds are some badge of honor or something. I think that it's just putting everyone in her mix.

Mystique asks, "Drama, which video do you like best?"

"Since I'm not in either of them, I don't like either one. BUT, if I must pick one, I pick the first one. Sam and Sunday's kiss is hot. I likes."

Dreya smiles at me as if something's changed. I don't know if it's because Truth is gone back to the States or if she's looking at me and Sam and likes what she sees. But this time, I think Dreya is really done. I think she's ready to move on without Truth to see what that looks like.

And that is definitely a good look.

28

When we get back to Atlanta from Barbados, the limo drops me and Sam off at my front door. He was going to go home, but I guess he's not tired of my company yet. This is a good thing because I'm not tired of his either. After our four-day excitement-filled weekend, it's good to be back home.

"You just go in," Sam says. "I'll get all of your stuff."

"Thank you, Sam."

He kisses my cheek. "You're welcome."

I feel warm on the inside as I float to my front door. Well, I'm not literally floating, but you know what I mean. I can barely feel my feet touch the ground. I'm glad Dreya went home in another limo, because I don't need her raining on my crush parade right now.

Before I get to the door, Manny throws it open. He has on *Transformers* pajamas although it's early in the evening. I could almost bet money that he's had them on all day.

"Sunday's home! Sunday's home on Sunday!" Manny giggles. "I know my days of the week. I think Auntie Shawn should've named you Saturday, because that one has the most letters!"

I grab him up and give him a hug. "Did Aunt Charlie teach you the days of the week?"

"Naw. Dora and Diego taught me. I can say them in Spanish too."

I carry him into the house and stop dead in my tracks in the living room. It's a disaster area in here. There are tubs and boxes everywhere. Packages of pillows, sheets, and blankets are stacked up against the wall, and storage containers are stacked on another one.

"Mom!" I yell. "What's going on in here? Is Aunt Charlie finally moving?"

Aunt Charlie pops up from behind one of the stacks. "Ha ha, heifer. I ain't going nowhere!"

"Rats!" I say.

Aunt Charlie throws a pillow at me. "Shawn, you better come get this girl before she gets hurt. Think she grown because she been to another country."

"I do not think I'm grown because I've been to another country. I think I'm grown because I'm *eighteen*!"

"Ooh, you and Dreya sure are smelling yourselves. Where is she anyway? She said she was coming here after the trip."

"I think she went home."

I know she went home because she doesn't want Aunt

Charlie to see the handprints around her neck from where Truth choked her. She won't be able to hide the fact that he was in Barbados, though, once the reality show comes on, but I'll let her be the one to tell Aunt Charlie.

My mom comes up from the back of the house and gives me a hug. "How was your trip? Did you take pictures?"

"Yes, I have lots of pictures. I wish it never ended. I've never had so much fun in my life."

Sam opens the door with his foot and he's got both hands and arms full of my stuff and his. "A little help?" he says.

I rush to relieve him of some of the bags. Even Manny comes and takes something from Sam.

"Thanks, Manny," he says. "Us men have to stick together."

Manny looks Sam up and down. "You don't know me like that. When are you going home? We up in here with our pajamas on."

My mom says, "Boy, go sit down somewhere. You are the only one in the house with pajamas on."

"My mommy ain't give me no clothes today!"

OMG! I knew it. Aunt Charlie is straight-up trifling when it comes to Manny. She cares more about what's on TV than what is going on with her baby.

"Oh hush, boy," Aunt Charlie says.

My mom says, "Sunday, I'm so glad you're home. You can tell me if you like this stuff or if I need to take it back to the store."

"This stuff is for me?" I ask.

She nods. "Aren't you the one going away to Spelman in three weeks?"

"It is only three weeks! Where in the heck did my summer go?"

"Let's see," my mom says. "You've been on a tour, you've been in the studio and you've been to the Caribbean. You've been pretty busy."

"I know. And the week before school starts I have to fly out to New York to premiere my video on *106 & Park*."

My mom says, "Well, that's fine because I got everything you need for your dorm. I had to do something . . . to keep my mind occupied."

Anytime my mom gets super upset she has to do something to stay busy. Whether it's cooking, cleaning, shopping, or whatever. I should be glad there's not more stuff here! With Carlos going to jail I'm sure she was beyond super upset.

"Well, I like it all fine enough, but I think BET has a sponsor that wants to decorate my dorm as part of the reality show. They hired an interior decorator and everything."

"Isn't that just perfect!" my mom says. "I guess I better go looking for the receipts."

"No, wait! Don't take it back. Sam is moving to New York City, so he could use all of this stuff . . . except maybe the purple comforter."

Sam says, "I like purple. Just kidding."

"Sam is moving to New York?" Aunt Charlie asks. "For what?"

"He's going to work at Epsilon Records as an in-house producer for Zillionaire's record label."

My mom gives Sam a hug. "Congratulations, Sam! I know Sunday was looking forward to spending time with you on the Georgia Tech campus, but this is a great opportunity for you."

"I'm going to go to Fordham University part-time while I work for Epsilon, so I'm still doing the college thing."

"How did Dilly take the news about his brother?" my mom asks.

"You know, he really didn't seem too twisted."

My mom smiles. "Then I'm sure Dilly will be okay."

And if he's not okay, Bethany will be there to help him get through it. She's been stuck to him like glue ever since we left the island. I don't even think she wanted to go home when we got back to ATL.

"You and Dreya think y'all slick," Aunt Charlie says.

"What are you talking about?"

She stands up and paces through the maze of boxes. "I'm sitting up here wondering when you were gonna tell me that Truth brought his trifling tail to Barbados."

"Wh-what?" How in the heck does she know?

"I bet you're guessing how I know. I gots me a snitch in your little crew and she tells me everything. Don't worry about who it is, 'cause I ain't telling you anyway. But she lets me know all the foolishness that happens with y'all."

I don't know how much she knows, so I'm not giving

her any extra information. "Okay, so your spy told you he was there. He was in Barbados, but not by my invitation. That had nothing to do with me."

"Didn't Epsilon Records pay for that whole trip?"

"They didn't pay for Truth. He paid his own way. Got his own plane ticket and room."

Aunt Charlie looks me up and down. "You're not gonna tell me the whole story, huh?"

"I don't exactly know what story you're looking for. Maybe you should call Dreya," I say. She's not about to be interrogating me for Dreya's stuff. I don't have anything to do with any of that mess.

Aunt Charlie says, "I don't need to call Dreya because I already know."

"What exactly do you know?" I ask.

"See, Shawn! That's what I'm talking about. She and Dreya are sneaky as what! I know she and Truth got into a fight, and somebody beat him down and knocked him out. Was it you, Sam? I didn't take you for much of a fighter, but I guess you could go if you had to."

I shake my head. "Don't answer that. This is Dreya's business, not ours. Come on, Sam, can you help me bring my bags to my room?"

Manny's eyes widen. "Um . . . wait, Sunday. . . . Before you go in there . . . what had happened was . . ."

I don't wait for Sam to bring the bags. I storm back to my room as if someone told me there was a sack of a million dollars waiting for me, but I had to get it in thirty seconds or less.

The scene in my room is horrific. My jaw drops off the

hinges when I see the inside of a teddy bear exploded all over my bed and carpet, hundreds of Happy Meal toys all over the floor, what can only be a jelly sandwich stuck to the ceiling, AND it smells like pee!

I let loose a growl that sounds like a tiger who just stepped on a tack. "MOM!!!"

29

Tonight, since Manny jacked up my bedroom, I'm sleeping on the living room couch. I'm way too tired to clean my room tonight and Aunt Charlie is not going to do it, even though it's her baby that made the mess. Just plain old triflin'.

Sam and I cleared an area in all of the boxes and containers so that I can at least see the TV. He's chilling like he doesn't want to go home.

"Doesn't your mother want to see you since you've been gone for four days?" I ask. His car has been parked in our driveway the entire weekend, so it's not like anyone has to take him home.

"She does, and I want to see her, but I'm afraid."

"Of what? Your mama?"

Sam chuckles. "No. I'm afraid of what my mama is gonna do when she finds out I'm going to move to New York. She's gonna trip out."

"But why? You're gonna go to school, so she should be okay with it."

Sam shakes his head. "Not my mother. I mean, you've met her. She thinks I'm a baby when it comes to living in another city. She was super happy when I said I was going to Georgia Tech."

"Do you want me to go with you when you tell her?" I ask, even though I'm not sure I want to be anywhere near that conversation.

"Nah. I'll do it on my own. "If I'm not man enough to face my mother, then I shouldn't be moving out on my own, right?"

"I guess."

A loud pounding on the door scares the daylights out of me. Sam and I jump up at the same time. I hope it's not some thugs trying to get revenge for what Carlos did to Bryce.

"Mama!"

That wail belongs to only one person. Dreya.

I run to the door and open it. Dreya's entire mouth is bloodied! She grabs hold of me and melts into my arms.

"Who did this?" I ask.

"Some girls . . ."

Why do I not believe this? "Aunt Charlie!" I yell.

Aunt Charlie and my mom come up from their bedrooms. When Aunt Charlie sees Dreya, she screams. She runs to me and takes Dreya into her own arms like we're passing a newborn baby.

"That punk did this to you, didn't he?" Aunt Charlie asks.

Dreya shakes her head. "The . . . the limo took me

home, and I got unpacked. Then, I wanted a Sl-slush from Sonic, and I was leaving my apartment. And s-some hoodrat girls jumped on me."

"Oh my goodness," my mother says. "I'm calling the police. This is assault."

Aunt Charlie looks at Dreya's neck. "Well, where did these bruises come from? They aren't fresh!"

Dang . . . all those episodes of *Law & Order* and *CSI* got Aunt Charlie sleuthing like some kind of forensic blood-splatter analyst.

"I don't know what you're talking about. Some girls just jumped me," Dreya says.

Aunt Charlie ignores Dreya's weak explanation and looks at me. "Sunday . . ."

"Why y'all always got to bring me in it? She told you what she wanted you to know."

My mother says, "Dreya and Sunday. Y'all better stop playing games. This is serious, now."

Sam stands up. "I don't know why y'all are protecting that fool. Ms. Charlie, Truth choked your daughter when we were in Barbados. Zac handled him, but it happened too quickly to keep him from putting his hands on Dreya."

Aunt Charlie removes her arms from Dreya and waves her fist at the sky. "That . . ."

The rest of her monologue is full of bad language. I mean . . . Auntie Charlie is mad!

My mom says, "Charlie, calm down. Dreya, are you sure Truth didn't do this to your face?"

"He didn't, Auntie Shawn. I wouldn't lie about this."

My mother frowns. "At this point, I don't know what

you would lie about. Come on. We're going to the police station."

Dreya howls at the top of her lungs. "I can't go to the police station with my face looking like this!"

"So you're not reporting it?" Aunt Charlie asks. "I know that Truth had something to do with this."

"Me too!" I say. "You're stupid if you keep letting him do this to you. How many injuries do you need to get?"

"Sunday, can you just call Big D?" Dreya asks.

"He's not the police."

Aunt Charlie says, "Dreya, I'm not playing with you. You obviously came here because you didn't know what to do with yourself, so we're going to help you. You're going to press charges and you're going to get a restraining order on Truth. Period. No more discussion."

Rarely does Aunt Charlie put her foot down about anything, but this time, I can tell she's serious.

"Well, I don't want them to come with me," Dreya says, pointing at me and Sam.

"Okay!" I say. "I don't have to come with you. I don't know why you're trying to dog me. I'm not the one who delivered you a beatdown."

My mom says, "Sunday, that's enough. Dreya is stressed out right now. Me and Charlie are taking her in. Just stay here and take care of Manny, okay?"

I nod. Of course, I'll take care of my cousin. I'm the one always trying to do the right thing.

I watch as my mother and Aunt Charlie take Dreya by each of her arms and lead her out of the house. I feel so torn, because part of me is angry that Truth would go this far to get back at Dreya, and the other part of me is done caring about Dreya's mess when she doesn't want my concern.

"You do know that Truth might not have anything to do with this latest beatdown, right?" Sam asks after they leave. "He's probably too worried about his music career to still try and get at Dreya."

"Who else would do that to Dreya?"

"As foul as she is, she's got to have some other enemies."

I think of the other person who is Dreya's archenemy. "Bethany . . . but I don't think it could've been her. She's happy that she and Dilly are back together."

"Well, whoever it was, it looks like Truth is going to get blamed."

I try to make myself feel sorry for Truth that he might be getting blamed for a crime that he didn't commit. Then I think about his hands wrapped around Dreya's neck in that limo, trying to hurt her, and I just can't make myself feel any sympathy.

Imagine that.

30

Sam and I are at Big D's studio to have a meeting about my record release. It's pretty tense in the room, because Sam's chilling at the boards adjusting and readjusting the equipment like this is the last time he's gonna touch it. Big D has this big old sad face looking like somebody stole his puppy.

And we're supposed to be celebrating! My record is coming out in a week! Somebody ought to be pumped up in here besides me.

I squeal as I see my album cover on Amazon.com. "It's here, Big D! Epsilon put it up today like they said they would. The cover art is slamming! It looks so much better than the mock-ups they sent us by e-mail."

Sam leaves the instruments and looks over my shoulder. "What's your Amazon rank?" he asks.

"I don't know! Where do I see that?"

"Scroll down," Sam says.

"Oh . . . it's four hundred. That's bad, huh?" I look at Big D, hoping he has something assuring to say.

"Actually, since they just put the album up less than an hour ago, that's good. You need to go on your Twitter page and let your fans know it's there."

I open another Internet tab, go to Twitter.com, and post, *My record is on Amazon.com!! Woo-hoo. Please help me get my rank up into the top ten!*

"Now we wait," Big D says. "But you've got a good number of followers."

"Mystique has like five million."

"You will too," Sam says. "Just wait and see."

Big D pats me on the shoulder. "Mystique didn't start off on top, baby. You've got to crawl before you walk."

I love Big D's pep talks. He keeps it all-the-way real. "You're right, Big D. I know I've still got a lot of work to do to reach her status. I'm gonna work it out though."

"I know you are, baby girl. Now go ahead and refresh that browser."

I click the F5 button on my laptop to refresh the screen. I look down at my status again, and I've moved from four hundred on my Amazon rank to nineteen. In minutes I shot all the way up.

"Does this mean I've sold a lot of records already?" I ask.

"It means that people are placing pre-orders, because the music isn't available yet," Big D says. "They're on your tip, baby girl. You should be happy!"

"I'm amazed, actually," I say.

This entire journey with recording my first record feels completely like a dream sequence. Having a record deal seemed to be the most impossible thing that could ever happen to me, then going on tour was impossible! Then, filming a video in Barbados, of all places. Impossible!

"Don't be amazed," Sam says. "You're amazing."

"I've got a surprise for you, Sunday. I was gonna wait until everyone was here later, but I think this is a perfect time for it."

Big D reaches into a cardboard box under his keyboard, and pulls out a CD. I see the pink and immediately start screaming! It's my CD! I'm wearing pink and khaki on the cover (like Dreya complained about), and my hair is in big loose waves framing my face. I've got on my bracelet with the S charm that Sam bought me months ago. In big bright letters it says *Sunday*. A self-titled record! That's what's up!

Epsilon Records was a little on the fence about calling the album *Sunday*, but Mystique convinced them that it would help with my brand recognition to come out the gate with a self-titled CD. Yeah, I don't know exactly what that means, but I trust Mystique when it comes to brand recognition. The entire world knows who she is!

"Look Sam! Look!"

Sam chuckles and takes another CD from Big D. "You look hot on here, Sunday. Just like a diva. I'm glad I got you before you blew up. I probably would've had to wait in line behind all the other dudes tryna holla."

"Can I take one to my mom?" I ask.

"The whole box is yours," Big D says. "They're your free copies."

Sam pulls the insert out of the CD cover and unfolds it. "Let's see who she thanks."

"Everybody!" I say with a laugh.

Sam reads, *"First, I want to thank God, who is the head of my life. I would like to thank Big D for discovering my talents and Mystique for putting me on the map. I couldn't do any of this without my mother, Shawn Tolliver. She holds it down for me at all times. Speaking of family, Aunt Charlie, Manny, and Dreya, much love forever! To my boo and bestie, Sam."*

He stops reading.

And laughs.

"Boo and bestie?" he asks.

"Hey, Big D had me writing that at like the last minute or something. I couldn't think of anything else!"

Sam continues, *"To my boo and bestie, Sam, you rock. Your talent inspires me. You are my muse. I would also like to thank Mystical Sounds and Epsilon Records for doing the do, and pulling out all the stops. Appreciate y'all. Last but not least, I want to thank my fans! Can't do this without you. Come ride with me all the way to the top of the Billboard charts! Much love, Sunday xoxo!"*

"Aw, Sunday," Sam says, "that was cute. I'm so happy to be your boo and your bestie."

"I'm never going to live that down, am I?"

Sam looks at the ceiling and then back at me. "Um . . . no."

Big D says, "Congratulations, Sunday. You deserve it."

Sam grabs a Sharpie off the counter and holds out the CD. "I want the first autographed copy of your CD!"

I can't help but smile as I take the CD from Sam's hand. "Okay . . . let's see. . . . What do I want to write.

To my boo and my bestie . . . Sam. . . . Do you, and continue to reach for the stars, so you can pluck down one for me. Much love, Sunday."

"Much love?" Big D chuckles as he asks his question. "You two are funny. Both too proud to admit that you're totally gone for each other. I'm going to enjoy dancing at your wedding."

Wedding? Okay, Big D has seriously hit the fast-forward button. I am not marrying anybody until I finish college, make a million, pass the bar. . . . Oh dang, I've got a lot of stuff I'm trying to do before I walk down anybody's aisle.

Sam's in for a loooonnnnng wait! I hope he's up for it.

"Why don't you hit refresh again!" Sam says. "Let's see where you are now."

I click the F5 button once more and guess what? I'm number eight.

Big D sits on his keyboard stool, and grabs his head. "You went into the Amazon.com top ten in the first hour of posting on Amazon.com, and you're not even released yet."

"That's really good, right?" I ask.

"Sunday, that's beyond good. That's incredible! You need to go home and celebrate with your mother," Big D says. "Ms. Tolliver is going to be so happy."

"She is, Big D. She's going to be ridiculously happy."

No one will be more thrilled 'bout this CD than my mother. Her losing my college fund was the catalyst to this entire journey. Like, I probably wouldn't have even stepped out and wrote that one hook for Truth if I hadn't been thinking of a way to raise money for my tuition.

It was a tragic situation turned into something good. Funny how things can happen that way. I wonder what good will come of the tragedy between Dreya and Truth. Maybe the good won't happen right away, but I think that eventually it will. Only time will tell.

Wait. Is that the title to a song?

31

When I get home, my mom is dressed to go out. She's got on a tiny black mini dress and some heels, and her hair is in a pretty, feminine roller set. My mom is flyer than the average mom!

"Where are you going?" I ask.

She laughs. "I don't have to tell you, do I?"

"No, but if you don't want me to have some of Big D's *associates* stalk you, then you better 'fess up!"

"Girl, please. I'm going on a date. With my coworker, Jimmy."

Oh! So Jimmy moved up from first-date to second-and-third-date status. Okay then, Mr. Jimmy. I see you!

"Where are y'all going?" I ask.

"Nosy!"

I stand there with eyebrows raised, waiting for my answer! I'm not playing on this.

My mother laughs again. "If you must know, with your nosy behind, we're going to the Luckie Lounge."

What? People that I know go to the Luckie Lounge. There are some folk there my mama's age, but there's a lot of young people too. I can't have any of my friends seeing my mama drop it like it's hot in the club! No way!

"Umm . . . I would appreciate it if y'all would select another venue. A more mature venue!"

"Sunday, you better go on somewhere with that! Jimmy's cousin is one of the bouncers there so we can get in for free. And they play my kind of music in there."

"Yeah, they play a lot of old-school rappers like Biggie and Tupac."

My mother tosses her head back and laughs hard, making her pretty curls shimmy like a waterfall. "Biggie and Tupac are not old school! Y'all kids are funny."

I shrug. They're old school to me. I was a little kid when they were on the charts. I can't even say I remember any of their songs.

"Are you gonna start kicking it hard, now that I'm moving out and going to college?" I ask.

I cannot imagine my mom, who has always been a homebody, suddenly hitting the club circuit. I mean she's fly enough to fit in just fine, but I don't know if I want that. Especially with me becoming a celebrity and everything. I don't want any guys trying to hit on my mama, so they can get at my money! Or worse, people coming up to my mama in the club, and giving her demos of them singing and rapping. All bad!

"I'm going to kick it if I want to, Sunday. You, Dreya,

and Charlie do exactly what you want to do, so I'm going to do me. Who's gonna check me, boo?"

OMG. She really needs to stop watching *Real Housewives of Atlanta*. For real. Wait! What if they ask my mom to be on that show? Her and Aunt Charlie's adventures are not ready for prime time. No thank you and no, ma'am.

I hand my mother a CD. "Well, this is what I wanted to show you before you go out kicking it!"

My mother takes the CD and turns it over in her hands. Tears spring to her eyes as she jumps up and down. "Oh my goodness! I mean, oh God's goodness! God is so good, Sunday. This is unbelievable!"

She wraps her arms around me and hugs me tight. I can barely breathe in her death grip, but it makes me feel happy nonetheless.

"When is the release date?" she asks.

"In seven days. The day after I go on *106 & Park*, to present my video."

"Sunday, you don't know how much I prayed and prayed when Carlos lost your college-tuition money. I asked God to make up the difference for my mistakes. And He's answered my prayer more than I could've ever hoped for."

"I know, Mom."

"I want you to remember that when things get rough," my mom says. "Because this is just the beginning, and it's gonna get rough. People are gonna be jealous of you, they're going to lie on you, and it's not always going to be fun."

I nod with understanding. I've already experienced some of this, mostly at the hands of my own cousin. But I know, the closer I get to the top, the hotter it's going to get. I think I'm ready. I hope I'm ready.

"I know, Mommy. But you're going to be praying for me, right? So, I don't have to worry too much."

My mother smiles and hugs me again. "Of course I'm going to pray for you, but you need to pray too. And keep people around you who you trust. Like Big D, Sam, and Mystique. They're all in your corner. I feel that about them."

"Well, what about Dreya? Shouldn't I keep her close too? You've always told me that family comes first. You always have Auntie Charlie's back."

The smile leaves my mother's face and she releases a long sigh. "I don't know what is going on with your cousin. She's not in a good place right now. As much as I tell you to have her back because she's family, I don't want you to get hurt in the process."

"I just think that if it really comes down to it, Dreya wouldn't do me harm. I have to believe that or I don't know how I could deal with all the crazy stuff that she does. I mean, like she's the closest thing I have to a sister."

"What I want you to do is pray for Dreya. I'm praying for her too, because as much as Truth has hurt her, I think she's still going to go back to him. I can tell that she's still not done with him."

"Why would she go back to someone who choked her?" I ask. "That's just crazy."

My mother says, "Yes, it is, but she refused to tell the

police officer that it was him. And the only way she could get a restraining order is if she presses charges."

"What makes her like that, Mom? Why is she holding on to him when he cheats and he's mean?"

"I don't know, but until she starts to value herself, there's nothing we can do about it."

The doorbell rings, and my mother's smile returns. "That's my date! You see how he doesn't just honk the horn? He's got some sense unlike some other people I know."

Those *other people* she's talking about are probably my dad and Carlos. I watch my mom get her pretty-girl swag on as she answers the door. Jimmy cheeses hard when he sees her, because like I said, my mother is fly!

"All right, Sunday. We'll celebrate your CD release in the morning with a pancake breakfast! Don't wait up for me."

Don't wait up for her? Oh, I see she really thinks that she's grown! She better be glad that I trust her not to do anything stupid or else she'd be on lockdown, house arrest, and all of the above.

But for real, though! I'm so happy my mother is smiling. She might just get that husband she's been waiting for all my life!

And Dreya . . . wow to her and her toxic relationship. I'm going to just do me. Go to New York, get my *106 & Park* on, release my video, and strive to be number one. I just hope that when I make it, I can look to the right of me and my sister-cousin will be there by my side.

Without her raggedy boyfriend.

32

I thought I was nervous the last time I was on *106 &
Park*, but this time I'm dang near mortified. We're pre-
miering both videos today on the show and the viewers
are going to pick which one gets put into rotation. Mystique told me that no matter which video the fans choose,
Epsilon Records has already selected video number one.
It seems they liked the kiss too. Apparently, Mystique is
the only one who had a problem with it.

I'm backstage on the set and I hear the crowd going
crazy. Then I start tripping because I realize that the
screaming is for me! There's nobody here with me, it's me
doing my own thing—Sunday Tolliver, pop star.

Sam is with me, because, well, he lives in New York
City now. Zac had offered his own crib to Sam while he
was getting settled, but Sam insisted on getting his own

spot. He didn't want to seem like one of Zac's entourage. I like that in him.

"You look good, Sunday," Sam says as he runs a hand over my high ponytail.

"It's okay? I don't look too teenybopper?" I ask. I'm feeling some kind of way about this ponytail, and I can't say that it's a good feeling.

"Who do you hear out there screaming but a bunch of teens? It's okay if you look teenybopper, because that's what they are."

"Rocsi's talking now! It's almost time for me to go on."

On stage, Rocsi says, "Today we've got a special treat! We've got Mystical Sounds recording artist Sunday Tolliver here in the studio! She's going to introduce her brand-new video. Her album drops tomorrow, so make sure you go and cop that!"

On cue, one of the show's producers holds up a hand to me to let me know I've got three minutes.

"You'll do great out there, and then we can go out to lunch or something."

"Really? Where are you taking me?"

"I was thinking about Sylvia's in Harlem. I'm in the mood for some soul food."

"Listen to us, making lunch dates and stuff like grown folks."

Sam laughs out loud. "We are grown aren't we?"

"I guess so. But I don't feel grown. I feel like my mama can come and bust all this up at any time and put my butt on punishment."

"I know, right?" Sam says. "When I told my mother I was moving to New York, she *did* put me on punishment. Then she changed her mind when I told her I was going to be making close to six figures a year and a royalty percentage."

"That's really good coming out the gate, Sam. Most eighteen-year-olds aren't making that kind of money."

"Well, most eighteen-year-olds don't have an investment broker either. I'm not playing games, Sunday. When we graduate college, I want us to have a life together."

I give Sam my big wide-eyed blank stare. "After we graduate college? I can't even think past next week, let alone four years from now."

"But I'm a planner, that's what I do. I just want you to know that I'm planning for us."

I gulp and hope Sam doesn't hear me or see the fear in my eyes. Why would he lay this on me right before I go out on stage? We just got to solid boyfriend/girlfriend status and now Sam wants to skip to forever? He stays on fast-forward, but he wouldn't be Sam if he didn't.

When the producer gives me the signal to go onstage, Sam squeezes my hand. It feels like something a fiancé would do. I shudder at the thought of it, feel myself getting cold feet, cold toes, and every other frozen extremity.

I'm walking in a daze, and now Rocsi has a microphone in my face. "So Sunday, you shot the video for 'Can U See Me' in Barbados? That's extra hot for a first video!"

"Yeah, it was incredible! We had so much fun."

"And you didn't just film a video, you filmed a reality show too, right?"

I nod. "Yes, the first episode of it is tonight on BET at nine o'clock!"

"Tell us, is there going to be lots of drama?"

I laugh out loud. "Yes, my cousin is on the show."

The crowd and Rocsi burst into laughter. "Your cousin does have an appropriate name, right?"

More laughter and cheers from the crowd. And someone yells, "I love you, Sunday!"

"I love you BACK!" I say in the microphone.

Rocsi laughs some more. "So there's something special going on with this video premiere, right? Tell the fans about it."

"Well, we actually shot two videos and we want the fans to pick the one you like the best. That's the one going into rotation on BET."

"I've seen them both, and they're hot! And isn't . . . isn't that the guy from the YouTube video playing your leading man? Is he your boyfriend?"

I smile. "Now, Rocsi, you know I don't talk about my personal life at all."

"Mystique has taught you well, I see."

"She is my mentor, you know."

"Well, Sunday, go ahead and announce your video!"

I take the microphone from her hand and say, "First, I want to give a shout-out to one of my fans. Her name is Zoey and she was going through a breakup when she heard this song. Zoey, I hope everything is going well for you. Whether you have a new guy or not, you are still super fab in my book! I'm dedicating this video premiere to you. This is both versions of 'Can U See Me'! I hope you enjoy it."

Both videos play on the big screens, and the crowd goes wild. Seeing it larger than life is a heart-stopping moment for me! And I just want to disappear when everyone hoots as Sam kisses me on-screen. I hope they can't tell that I'm blushing, because all the evasiveness in the world won't be enough if I'm red as a firecracker when the lights go back up.

After the video plays, Rocsi says, "Right after the break, Sunday is gonna sing her single 'Inbox Me' live!"

Backstage I drink a warm bottled water and take a potty break before it's time for me to sing. Even though "Inbox Me" is not my favorite track off the album, I still plan to rock it all the way live.

When I hit the stage again, all nervousness and embarrassment about being kissed on-screen is gone and it's all about the performance. All about hitting the right notes, all about making it hot.

Because that's what I do. I make it hot!

I hear the intro play and I start singing, *"Inbox me/Don't want everyone to know-ow-ow/Inbox me/Get up on this dance floor/Inbox me/Don't leave it on my wall/Inbox me/You don't even have to call . . ."*

This is my first radio single, and although it didn't quite make it to number one on the chart, it did break the top five, which is fabulous for a newcomer like me! I told them that "Can U See Me" was a better single, but Epsilon chose to listen to Mystique instead.

We'll see who's right when "Can U See Me" hits number one on the Billboard charts. And I know it will! With the reality show and two hot videos to back it up, this song is going straight to the top.

And my career is going with it! Sunday Tolliver—chart topper! It has a great ring to it. No . . . it has a fab ring to it!

33

EPSILON RECORDING ARTIST DRAMA GETS BEAT-DOWN IN THE HOOD (pictures inside).

I blink rapidly as I read the Mediatakeout.com headline. I'm afraid to click the link. How could they have pictures? Who would do that?

But curiosity gets the best of me and I do click the link. The picture is bad. It's really, really bad. It had to have been taken right after those girls jumped on Dreya. And the only place she went was to the police station.

The story reads:

> Epsilon Recording artist Drama was jacked outside her Atlanta apartment two weeks ago. Snitches say that it is related to her ongoing beef with ex-boyfriend Truth, who was dropped from Epsilon Records after one album release—

for mysterious reasons. The pictures were sent to us from an anonymous e-mail account with a message for Drama. *Epsilon money can't protect you every day of your life. Watch your back, Drama. . . . We coming for you.* If anyone has any information on the goons that did this to one of our favorite new artists, please call the Atlanta police department. And we're praying for you, Ma!

Before I can read the article a second time my cell phone rings.

"Hello."

"Did you see it?" It's Mystique.

"Yeah, I saw it. It's bad. Dreya looks a mess in that picture."

Mystique says, "I know. She's gonna have a coronary."

"What should she do? Should she respond? Should she stay quiet? And what about the threat? Do you think that's real?" I ask a flurry of questions that suddenly occur to me.

"I think the threat is fake," Mystique says. "No matter how mad Truth is, he knows he can't mess up in the industry. There could be a lot of reasons why he got dropped from Epsilon. Nobody knows it's because Zac requested it."

"Zac got him dropped? Wow. I didn't know he liked Dreya all that much."

Mystique says, "I think it was more about Dilly than Dreya. He thinks that Dilly can go far, but that Epsilon needs to put more money behind him. Plus, Truth's album sales were just okay. The only hit song on the record was the one with your hook. It had a lukewarm response."

"So, just like that? One bad album release and you're out the door?"

"Yeah, Sunday. You didn't know? You're only as hot as your next project. If your first project sucks, then there won't be a number two. It's called a one-hit wonder."

"That's messed up."

"But you don't have to worry about that."

"Really? Why don't I?"

"Your SoundScan numbers for your first-week sales were 578,000. You went gold your first week! And your album debuted at number three on the *Billboard* pop chart!"

I almost drop the phone! "Get the heck out of here! So, I'm a millionaire!"

"Pretty much, baby! Welcome to the club!"

My mother and her prayers are like a powerful weapon. I mean, she carries those prayers around with her like the stuff Batman carries in that little fanny pack around his waist! She's prayed up a gold record and over a half million records sold!

OMG.

"Sunday! Are you there?" Mystique says.

"I'm here! I am. I just can't believe this is happening. Every time something new comes up, I just can't believe it!"

Mystique giggles. "You better start believing it, girl! I told you that you are more than a one-hit wonder. You're set to be an icon!"

This makes me think of the future. A future of living a

fabulous life! A future of getting my mother off of her job, out of this neighborhood, and into a gated community. A future of my little cousin Manny going to private schools and getting the best education his little grown self can handle.

But there's no way I can visualize the future without putting Sam in the picture!

34

"I can't believe it's finally here! My first day of college."
I'm having a confessional right on the Spelman campus.
There's a whole camera crew and not just our regular camera dude. I think they want to get a lot of shots of the school and students, to make this episode really pro-education.

"It's ironic, because I wouldn't even be in this music industry thing if it wasn't for me trying to get to college. And now, I'm finally here."

"How are you feeling about Sam not being here in ATL with you?" the producer asks.

"Well, it's hard not having my best friend here with me. We were planning to have a lot of fun off-campus. But he's getting his grind on, and I can't hate him for that. It's all about the come up."

The camera crew follows me as I try to make heads or tails of this campus map. My mom was going to take off work to come with me, but she has a fear of being on TV.

She thinks that the TV makes her look fatter than she really is. I keep telling her that all those pots of spaghetti are making her look fatter, but anyway.

I'm staying in the Stewart Living & Learning Center! It's the only residence hall with upperclassmen too. And it's for all of us extra-smart honors students. Score!

"Here it is!" I say out loud although I'm not talking to anyone in particular.

The other girls on campus are staring at me, or maybe at the crew of cameramen that are following me. This is gonna be a little bit weird, I think. But as soon as I'm able to ditch the cameras, I think it'll be easier.

I walk into the residence hall and find my room, which is on the second floor. It's a double-occupancy room, so I get a roommate! I'm looking forward to this. I hope she'll be cool, smart, and funny, and I hope she doesn't mind having to share a room with a pop star.

I use my key card to open the door, and I squeal at how the room has been decorated. There's not a stitch of Ikea furniture in here! This is all top of the line. My bed has a huge purple comforter with fringes and white pom poms. It's totally something my mom would've picked for me, even though I'm not a girly girl.

My roommate is here too. She's looking me up and down with a little smile on her face.

"Are you kidding me? I got the reality star?" she says.

It takes a half second for me to realize that she's kidding, and we both burst into laughter. "Hi, I'm Sunday Tolliver," I say.

"Well everyone knows who you are! I'm Gia Stokes. Nice to meet you."

Gia looks like she's gonna be a buttload of fun. She's got this huge afro with a butterfly clip holding it up on the side. She's super tall and thin—model thin. And even though she doesn't have on a stitch of makeup she looks camera ready.

She's gorgeous. I hate her! Just kidding.

"I guess having an interior designer is one of the perks of having a star for a roommate. Are there any other ones?" Gia asks. She motions to the cameras. "Are *they* one of the perks?"

I laugh out loud. "No. They'll be gone after today."

"Cool, cool. Well, I'll let you settle in. Do you want something to eat? I'm going to grab something from Jack in the Crack."

"Sure! A burger would be great."

I watch Gia sashay past the cameras with her heeled sandals on. Strut, girl! But then she stumbles and nearly falls. She catches herself, and then turns to look at the cameraman.

"Make sure that doesn't wind up on TV. I'm trying to preserve my pretty-girl swag."

I crack up laughing. This chick is hilarious! I already can tell we are going to be great friends. She leaves the room and closes the door behind her.

Then two seconds later, she pops her head back in. "Spelman, baby!" she yells.

This makes me burst into a full-on belly laugh. Yeah, this year is gonna be great. College is so going to rock. And I'm doin' it big-money, college-pimpin' style!

Spelman, baby!

DOING MY OWN THING

Nikki Carter

ABOUT THIS GUIDE

The following questions are intended to
enhance your group's reading of
DOING MY OWN THING.

Discussion Questions

1. Was Sunday right to invite her crew on her tour? Was it a good or a bad decision?

2. Was Sam being unreasonable when he wanted a commitment from Sunday?

3. Is Dreya the villain of the story, or does she really have Sunday's back?

4. If you were Dreya, would you have forgiven Truth? Why or why not?

5. Do you believe that Bethany has truly turned over a new leaf? Is she a good match for Dilly, or should he find another girl before he gets hurt?

6. How did you feel when Sunday met up with her father? Should she have made a different decision about him?

7. Did Sunday give the correct advice to her fan Zoey whose boyfriend broke up with her on Facebook? Has that ever happened to you? How did you feel?

8. What were your thoughts on Shawn's advice to Sunday about Dreya? Should she just pray for her cousin or continue to hold it down for family?

9. Do you think that Sunday and Sam will survive a long-distance relationship?

10. Will Sunday and Gia make good roommates? Do you think they're compatible?

Nikki Carter Interview Questions

Q. Nikki, you seem to really like reality shows! Which ones are your favorites?

A. *Real Housewives of Atlanta* is my favorite! I used to watch *Flava of Love* too. Beyond hilarious.

Q. So who would win in a fight, NeNe or Kim?

A. NeNe. All day and all night. Hands down.

Q. Who has more pretty-girl swag, Nicki Minaj or Lil' Kim?

A. Well . . . Lil' Kim has grown-lady swag. She's got nothing to prove! But Nicki Minaj is a beast! It's a TIE!

Q. Who are your top-five favorite rappers?

A. Nas, Eminem, Drake, Jay-Z, and the late, GREAT Notorious B.I.G.

Q. No Diddy?

A. Wasn't the question about rappers? He's a mogul . . . not a rapper!

Don't miss Nikki Carter's

All the Wrong Moves,

available now wherever books are sold!

"Come on, Sunday. Give it your all. I know you can push this song out."

I take a deep breath and close my eyes. Maybe it's the fact that I'm recording my very first single on my very first album that's got me totally twisted.

Maybe it's the fact that mega-super R & B star Mystique is producing the song and is my mentor! Her words of encouragement are not helping, even though she has a smile on her face.

Mystique continues, "Sunday, I know you've got it in you. I've heard you sing the mess out of this song. Do you need me to leave?"

I shake my head no.

"Do you want me to come in the booth with you?"

I cock my head to one side and shrug. I don't know if that will help, but at this point I'm willing to try anything because I'm tired, hungry, and thirsty.

Sam, the recording engineer and my sort-of crush says over the microphone, "I'm taking a break. Y'all let me know when you're ready."

I feel the tension leave my body when Sam walks out of the recording room. Oh no! That's it! Sam is the reason I can't get this song right.

"Talk to me, mama," Mystique says as she steps into the tiny recording booth. "You seem a little stressed today."

I play with my ponytail nervously. "I-I don't know what it is."

Mystique smiles. "I think you know what it is, and you don't want to tell me."

"Okay . . . maybe you're right."

"Does it have anything to do with that video on You-Tube?"

I sigh at the thought of that video. It was the night of rapper Truth's release party at Club Pyramids, here in Atlanta. It was a hot mess of an evening.

Sam was pissed because I wouldn't be his "official girl," so he was tripping and dancing all crazy on some groupie chicks. Truth, who goes out with my cousin Dreya, took that as his opportunity to push up on me yet again, even though I'd told him no a hundred times. But since Sam was acting a fool with the groupies, I acted an even bigger fool and danced with Truth, knowing that Sam would flip the heck out.

And he definitely flipped out.

He bloodied Truth's face up right before his show, and although the concert went on, the fight was the biggest news of the night. Somebody had used the video camera on his phone to capture the whole thing.

It was on YouTube before we even got home that night.

Ever since then, I've been trying to make it up to Sam. We're supposed to be going to prom together, but it's in three weeks and Sam still isn't speaking to me.

"I guess it has a little bit to do with the video," I admit to Mystique.

"Listen. You guys can't let that stuff get to you. If I got upset about everything that's on the Internet about me and my man, I'd never get any sleep."

"Yeah, but the blogs only have rumors about you! They don't have anything concrete. They've got video of me."

Mystique places a hand on my arm. "It's just your first lesson in being in the limelight. Just remember that someone is always watching."

"That's the problem! I don't know if I want that! I just want to be a normal teenager."

"There are pros and cons to being a celebrity. But I wouldn't trade it for anything, Sunday! I've traveled the world, met the president, and I have millions of fans who care about me. Do you know I got three hundred thousand birthday cards?"

I laugh out loud. "Wow! Really?"

"Yes. And you'll have the same thing. You're so talented, and I know you can do this."

"But this song . . . it's about a girl having a crush on a guy. It's just hard to do with Sam out there mean mugging me."

"Yeah, guys have pretty fragile egos. He's just hurt right now, I guess."

"But why the double standard? I didn't trip about his groupie chicks."

Mystique chuckles. "From what I heard you did trip! You danced with Truth? Girl, you know that was messy."

"It was messy, wasn't it?"

"Just talk to Sam. Admit you were wrong, and then maybe y'all can get back to being friends again."

"You think so?"

"Yeah, but I need you to do it quickly, so we can record this single."

Sam walks back into the studio and says over the mic, "You ready, Sunday?"

I glance at Mystique, and she nods. "Sam, I need to make a phone call. Can you hold on a sec?" she asks.

She winks at me on the way out of the booth and mouths, "Talk to him."

I bite my lip as I try to get up the courage to talk to Sam. He seems to be deep in thought as he plays what sounds like random notes on the keyboard. I know him, though, so it's not random. He's got a melody in his head.

I step out of the booth and ask, "Working on something new?"

"What? Oh, naw. Not feeling inspired too much."

"Lost your muse?" I ask.

That was an inside joke, but Sam doesn't laugh. We worked so well together writing the songs on Dreya's album that he'd started calling me his muse.

"Yeah, I guess so," he replies.

I clear my throat, trying to think of a way to start this

conversation. "Y'all video got twenty thousand hits on YouTube."

Sam gives me a crazy look. Why in the world did I say that? OMG! Open mouth and insert foot.

"Twenty thousand people saw me puttin' work in on Truth. Sweet."

"You're such a guy."

"Yeah. I am."

"You did kinda put a beat-down on him, though."

Sam frowns. "Wish I hadn't done it, though. It wasn't worth it."

"I wasn't worth fighting for?" I ask. "Wow."

"Well, why should I be fighting over a girl who doesn't want to be with me? That doesn't make a lot of sense."

"Sam, I never said I didn't want to be your girl."

"You never said you did."

This conversation is going in circles. "So, are we not friends anymore now? 'Cause I still want us to be friends, Sam."

"I guess we can be friends, but you're gonna have to give me a while to get over the whole thing with Truth. When I see him, I just want to punch him again."

"You can't do that! I need . . . I mean we need you on the tour."

"Y'all don't need me. I'm the studio engineer and producer. I can stay here over the summer."

I touch Sam's shoulder and feel him flinch. "Sam, can you imagine how crazy that's gonna be for me if I have to be on tour with Dreya, Truth, and Bethany, without you? As a matter of fact, I'm gonna pull out if you don't go."

"Are you crazy? You can't pull out of the tour. Mystique and Epsilon Records would trip."

"I'm not going unless you go."

"It's not that serious, Sunday."

"Yes, it is."

He sighs. "All right, cool. I'll go."

"Yay!" I kiss Sam on the cheek, and he flinches again. "Don't . . ."

"Friends don't kiss each other on the cheek?"

"I don't want your lips on me."

I give him a smart-aleck smirk. "That's not true. You soooo want my lips on you."

"Sunday, don't play with my emotions."

"Okay, I'll stop. But can I ask you one more thing?"

"What?"

"Are we still going to prom together?"

Sam puffs his cheeks with air and taps a few notes on the keyboard. I can tell he's trying to think of an answer.

"I mean, it's okay if you don't . . ." I say.

"It's not that I don't want to, but I got so angry with you that I asked another girl at my school to go to my prom."

"Oh." I blink a few times because I refuse to let a tear drop. He asked someone else? He could've told me before he did that. I thought we were better than that. I guess I was wrong.

"You didn't ask someone else?" he asks.

"No. I thought we'd make up by the time prom came."

"Do you still want me to go to your prom with you?"

I shrug. "If you want to, I guess. I don't have a date."

Sam flashes a bright smile. "Okay. We can go as friends."

"Right. As friends."

Mystique comes back into the recording room. "Are we ready to record now?"

"Yes," I reply. "Let's do this."